Who's Alvie Wybel?
...and Why Is He Living in my Attic?
(Book 1)

*To Jeanette
From Dar*

Other Books by this Author
Helmi

Pierce the Skies
(poems about birds of Michigan's Upper Peninsula)

Who's Alvie Wybel?
...and Why Is He Living in my Attic?
(Book 1)

Dar Bagby

Published by Dar Bagby

Copyright ©2021 by Dar Bagby

ALL RIGHTS RESERVED. No part of this publication may be reproduced, distributed, or transmitted in any form or by any means, including photocopying, recording, or other electronic or mechanical methods, without the prior written permission of the publisher, except in the case of brief quotations embodied in critical reviews and certain other noncommercial uses permitted by copyright law. For permission requests, contact publisher/author.
(darbagby@gmail.com)

Published by Dar Bagby
Cover photo is property of the publisher

Manufactured and written in the United States of America

First Edition
Printed in the United States of America

ISBN 13: 978-1-0879-3510-2

Library of Congress Control Number: 2020925335

This is a work of fiction. The characters and dialogue are drawn from the author's imagination and are not to be construed as real (with the exception of quotes where noted). The opinions in this book are the author's opinions only and are freely offered. They are not meant to be offensively portrayed.

DEDICATION
This book is dedicated to all persons whose lives were touched, in any way, by the twentieth-century Holocaust.

TABLE OF CONTENTS

Prologue 1
1908..7
1918..15
1926..29
1927..35
1928..47
1936..61
1942..73
1943 – January 89
1943 – February through June 101
1943 – July 111
1943 – To the End of the Year..125
1944..135
1945 – January through June 151
1945 – July through December 169
Endnotes...179

AUTHOR'S NOTE
Instead of footnotes, I have chosen to use endnotes to identify quoted material used in this story, as well as explanations of certain occurrences and/or descriptions of events and places throughout the areas where the action takes place. These are identified using super-scripts within the text of each chapter, and they correspond with the number in that chapter's name in the **ENDNOTES** section found at the back of the book.

*'Tis a fearful thing to love what death can touch.
A fearful thing to love, to hope, to dream, to be.*

Yehuda HaLevi (1075-1141)

PROLOGUE

Michigan's upper peninsula—the U.P., No Man's Land, God's Country, whatever people called it—was Rene's favorite place to be, an untamed land full of hearty lumbermen eager to fell the pine that filled its forests, and fishermen who risked their lives on the fierce waters of Lake Superior. Rene (whose given name was Irene) was born in 1889 during the prime of the logging industry. She was an only child and considered herself lucky to have been raised in Grand Marais (pronounced *grand muh-RAY*), a little dot of a town on Lake Superior's wild southern shore. It had been named nearly three centuries earlier by the French voyageurs.

Rene's ma and pop died within four days of one another when she was seventeen. Her pop had the cancer, and Rene was thankful the disease took him rapidly. The day he was buried, Rene's ma caught her heel in the hem of her dress while climbing out of the wagon, fell about three feet, and hit her head on the wheel hub. Two mornings later, Rene went into her ma's room to see why she wasn't up and doing her usual chores; she was cold when Rene touched her in her bed. Rene was suddenly alone, and she accepted it because she had to, just as all the people in Grand Marais accepted the hand they'd been dealt.

In its heyday during the mid-to-late 1880s, Grand Marais had a population of 3000. But by 1910 the town's prosperity, having been provided by the mighty pine for so many years, turned into a paltry compensation from commercial fishing, and the population dwindled to around 200. Despite their mandatory shift in occupation, however, the inhabitants were as pleasant and helpful to each other as folks could be, probably because they were forced to depend on one another for their livelihoods. And that included Emmo Vandersligh. Though he didn't live in Grand Marais, he came through town twice a week during the spring, summer, and fall on his rounds to deliver the ice that preserved Grand Marais's water-borne harvest, along with the needs of storekeepers, barkeeps, and the general public's ice boxes.

Emmo was a big, burly man with lots of bushy hair the color of oak leaves in autumn on both his head and his face. His hands were half the size of beaver pelts, and he stood over six feet tall. He didn't need to wear snowshoes in the winter because his feet were as flat and wide as a bear's paws. But his demeanor was like that of a kitten; he was soft-spoken and ready to be everyone's friend, no questions asked. He whistled like a bird, and that smile of his—big as the crescent-shaped harbor for which Grand Marais has always been renowned.

He owned an ice storage and delivery business located in Gulliver, a small town down on Lake Michigan, south-southwest of Rene's hometown. Emmo delivered ice to various individuals and businesses between Gulliver and Grand Marais, the latter being the final stop on his route. As was popular in the day, his ice wagon was brightly painted. It was canary yellow with a white top, and on both sides, in big red letters, was:

M.O. VANDERSLIGH

ICE

STORAGE & DELIVERY
GULLIVER, MICHIGAN

Two big, strong horses, Grog and Ivy, pulled his wagon. During the warm months, the wagon rolled along on wheels. But before the snow melted during the spring, or in autumn when several inches of the white stuff often fell before winter set in to stay, Emmo attached runners so the wagon could slide across the snow, making it easier for the horses to pull. There were bells on the horses' harnesses; thus, the wagon could always be heard coming, bells jingling and Emmo whistling.

When Rene was a child, Emmo's arrival twice a week was pure joy. All the kids in town would tag along beside the wagon as it came down Main Street. If he arrived when there was snow on the ground, the kids knew Emmo would have a stockpile of snowballs on the seat beside him, and they'd engage in a rousing snowball fight, them trying to knock him off his perch high up on the wagon and Emmo bombarding them from above.

Most of the people in Grand Marais were dwarfed by Emmo's stature. Rene, on the other hand, was not. When she was ten-and-a-half years old, she took a growing spurt and shot up just shy of seven inches in one summer! And she didn't stop growing until she reached five-foot-eleven when she was seventeen. She had no idea which of her relatives was responsible for providing the gene that made her so tall; her ma and pop were both small, her ma being only five-foot-one and her pop five-foot-six. She had never met her grandparents, but her ma and pop assured her they had all been people of average height, and a few precious photographs backed up that fact. When Rene stood up straight, she could almost look eye-to-eye with Emmo.

After her parents passed on, Rene immediately got a job cleaning and cooking at the boarding house/bar on the top of the hill. Most of Grand Marais's businesses had closed, one after another, until the only remaining ones were the commercial fishery, the boarding house, a general store, a post office (located inside the general store), a telegraph office, a livery with a blacksmith, a butcher shop, a doctor who also saw people for dentistry needs and even served as the town's veterinarian, one bank, a barber shop, a newspaper office that had two employees who published a two-sheet paper every other week, a lawyer's office that consisted of one attorney (who was pushing 60), and one church with both a minister and a priest who offered a protestant service and a mass on alternating Sundays. In addition, four bars existed in Grand Marais: an upscale and highly respectable one on the main floor of the boarding house, another that had a billiard table, one where all the men with a propensity for gambling played poker, and the fourth with a tiny raised platform in a corner where some of the musically talented members of the community took turns playing their instruments and/or singing for the bar's patrons on most Saturday nights. Rene was somewhat puzzled over the fact that, though the town was on a limited budget, there was never a shortage of alcohol.

There was also, by default, a school of sorts. The woman who lived adjacent to the boarding house possessed a vast library of books. People assumed she was well-read and, therefore, intelligent, so some of the men in town built a room onto her house, and that became the school. The woman agreed to be the teacher until a certified one could be coaxed into living in Grand Marais.

After getting the boarding house job, Rene closed-up the house in which she'd been raised and moved into the boarding house where she occupied the smallest room available. Her meals (which she cooked for both herself and the guests) were free, and she got to keep any tips she garnered by being exceptionally pleasant or funny or helpful to the people staying there. She wasn't concerned about high fashion, so she didn't spend much on clothes or shoes except what was necessary to keep herself warm in winter, cool in summer, and respectable at church. She had no interest in spending her money, only in saving it in case hard times came along and demanded that she use it.

Twice a week during the ice delivery seasons, Emmo stayed overnight at the boarding house. He spent most of his free time there in discussions with Grange Reiker; they had become great friends. Grange worked for a rail line out of Gladstone. He no longer traveled the rails but lived in one of the rooms in the boarding house, expenses paid by the railroad. He had lost his left forearm in an accident while coupling cars, but he was otherwise an asset to the company. Grand Marais was the termination point for their rail line, so Grange took care of the business there. The railroad had been built during the peak of lumbering in the U.P., but it had taken a backseat now that Grand Marais's only claim to fame was fishing. In fact, to the town's chagrin, it was rumored that their portion of the rail system was soon to be closed.

Grange was a voracious reader, consuming every bit of literature he could get his hands on. He especially liked to quote famous people, and he seemed to be able to offer up a quote for every occasion that arose. One of his favorites, and the one he most often quoted to visitors at the boarding house, was from a book he'd read about Martha Washington. She epitomized his own position: "I am still determined to be cheerful and happy in whatever situation I may be; for I have also learnt, from experience, that the greater part of our happiness or misery depends upon our dispositions and not upon our circumstances." Without a doubt, Grange's disposition proved Martha right.

Rene found herself smitten with Emmo, even though he was multiple years her senior. She made a point of keeping his room spic and span, and she always put fresh wildflowers in a vase on the nightstand when she knew he would be overnighting. She cooked his favorites for supper and breakfast, and in the evenings after her work was finished, she often sat with him and Grange in the lobby and listened to their wonderfully entertaining stories. She laughed at the appropriate times and added her opinions whenever asked. Evidently it all paid off because, two summers later, Emmo asked Rene to marry him. She said yes, and on a beautiful day in mid-October of 1908, she became Mrs. Maarten Octavian Vandersligh.

1908

"I DO"

Rene always loved cake, and in her estimation, there was no better cake than wedding cake—straight-up white cake with white icing, loaded with sugar, rich and smooth with lard, and absolute heaven on a fork. Her mouth watered just thinking about it. In the never-ending search for an answer to the question *Which is better, vanilla or chocolate?* vanilla always won in her book. She said, "It's plain, and it describes me perfectly. In all aspects of my life—appearance, values, desires—plain is appropriate."

In the mid-morning October sunshine, Pearl, Rene's best friend, was helping her cut flowers for the wedding bouquet. Pearl was barely four-foot-ten, and when she and Rene were together, it was a humorous sight to behold; everyone called them David and Goliath. It being autumn, there wasn't a lot of variety in bloom, so Rene decided on blue star flowers and goldenrod, since they were abundant on the sunny south side of her parents' house.

Pearl shook her head. "I don't understand why you didn't get some roses or gardenias from a florist. I'm sure there would be some at that flower shop over in Munising."

"I don't want to spend a lot of money on flowers when I have these beautiful ones at hand." Pearl gave her that look she always did when she knew there was no use trying to argue with her friend. "Besides," Rene said, "I think it's a nice sentiment that they'll represent something my mother loved so much."

Pearl blushed. "I hadn't thought of that. You're right. I wish she could be here to see you on such a special day."

Rene gave her a tender smile. "She's here," she said, tapping her chest over her heart. They continued to cut flowers, leaving the stems long so they could put them in water until it was time to trim them to length and tie them in a nice bunch, wrapping white ribbon around them just before Rene walked down the aisle.

At 1:30 p.m. Emmo and Rene stood before Reverend Walker. They were flanked by Pearl and Grange, and the pews were filled with townspeople. No family was present—neither of them had any. The reverend asked, "Do you, Irene, take Maarten to be your lawfully wedded husband?" And she said, "I do." She later admitted to Pearl, "That's the only part of the ceremony I remember."

Rene and Emmo didn't exchange rings; they merely repeated some words, and Rene didn't recall if they had been recited with or without emotion. Standing before God and a handful of Grand Marais's population, Rene's mind had wandered. *Both of us said we'd marry the other, but the names aren't what we call each other: according to Reverend Walker, Irene is marrying Maarten. But isn't it really that Rene is marrying Emmo? It almost seems fraudulent. I suppose it doesn't matter in the long run, though, because if Irene and Maarten are happy for years to come, then Rene and Emmo will be, too.* And the reverend said to Emmo, "You may now kiss the bride."

Following the ceremony, they all walked to the boarding house, ate some white cake with white icing, and chatted pleasantly with those in attendance. After about half an hour, Emmo and Rene climbed up onto the seat of Emmo's ice wagon, waved their good-byes, and headed south toward Gulliver. Several miles had gone by when Emmo said, quietly, "We haven't decided where we're going to live."

"I thought we were going to live at your place," Rene said dumbfoundedly.

"Well, of course that's where we'll stay until we get a place that's *ours*, not just *mine*." He looked at her, a big grin lighting his face.

Rene was beside herself with pride because she had saved up quite a bit of money during the two years she'd been working at the boarding house. She grinned back at Emmo and said, smugly, "We can probably get a nice place. After all, I'm sitting on a pretty little nest egg."

"Really?" he seemed surprised. "And would I be too forward if I asked how much you're talking about?"

"Well, I don't mean to brag, but I have nearly two-hundred dollars saved up."

His face went blank and his jaw dropped. Rene knew she'd impressed him! He blinked a few times, then he said, "Uh-huh. That's...something to take into consideration."

Rene didn't know what that meant. It was her turn to blink. "My parents' house is available, of course, but that wouldn't be beneficial for your work, considering you need to be where the ice storage warehouse is. Am I right?"

He just kept staring at her with that blank expression.

"I don't even know what condition the house is in, considering it's been boarded up for two years. I know all of their furniture is still there, so we wouldn't have to buy anything new, if that's something you want to consider. I mean, we could use it if you think we could transport it in your ice wagon." She'd thrown the ball into his court.

He reached over and squeezed her hand. "I am truly surprised that you were able to save some money for us. I'm certain that created difficulty for you."

"None at all," she assured him. "I've always been good at putting money aside in order to have the security of knowing I would not be derelict if I had no job for a spell."

"You're a smart woman, Rene Vandersligh."

She fought to repress the look of euphoria that was struggling to overtake her face at hearing him tell her she was smart, as well as hearing her married name coming from his lips.

"I've been saving, too," he said. "A bit more than you, since I've been working for more years, of course." Emmo was twenty-eight years older than Rene, making him forty-seven, which meant he had been working longer than she had been alive. And it suddenly occurred to her that her paltry savings of $192.33 was nothing compared to the amount she was sure he'd saved. Her face went crimson, and she removed her hand from his, averting her gaze to some obscure place between the here-and-now and somewhere out in the vast blue of the sky. Her moment of pride was leading her to that proverbial fall, and she was embarrassed at having been so self-satisfied only moments before.

"Have I done or said something to upset you?" Emmo asked, pulling on the reins and stopping the horses. He turned in his seat and looked at her. She willed herself to look back at him. His eyes were tender and showed an obvious amount of disquietude. His voice was low and soft. "I fear I have appeared to make your contribution to our future seem paltry. Please let me apologize if I inadvertently stepped on your toes."

"Oh, Emmo, you speak so eloquently. The apology should be mine." She closed her eyes in embarrassment. "I presumed to think that my small savings could possibly make a difference in the amount of funds we will need in our future. I failed to consider…"

He cut her off. "Rene, Rene, Rene." He took her by the shoulders, and she opened her eyes, knowing she had to meet his gaze. He looked deeply into her very soul. "I, too, have been saving money because, like you, I was not one to spend willy-nilly on unnecessary items—things I might enjoy for a brief moment and then cast aside. But I had no plans for my future, especially not a future with the woman of my dreams. I only saved because I had nothing better to do with my money. You, on the other hand, had a purpose in mind. That makes what you saved—every penny of it—worth far more than any amount I've compiled. I feel overwhelmed and…and…honored, even, to be the one who'll share the fruits of your labors. Please forgive me for taking your endeavor too lightly."

How am I supposed to react to that? she thought. She had no doubt that he was being totally honest about his deepest feelings, but she had never been on the receiving end of such sincerity. On the verge of tears, she squeaked, "I adore you." She was encountering pure, unadulterated pleasure and unmitigated relief, seeing as how he had just provided her with an insight into his true self.

He responded with a blank stare. Finally, he said, "You, my dear, are a joy to behold. How I wish I had recognized your openness, your receptiveness, years ago. Until you began working at the boarding house, I only saw you as a child…" He stopped short. Then he put his big arms around her, wrapping her in a bearhug, and he began to laugh. He threw his head back and guffawed as if Rene had just told him a great joke. It took nearly a full minute for him to belay his laughter. He fumbled around to remove a handkerchief from his pants pocket and wipe his eyes between spurts of giggling until he was once again able to speak. By that point, his hilarity had become contagious, and Rene was chuckling along with him.

"Oh, Emmo. Please tell me our life together will be filled with moments just like this one." She was still a bit confused about his reaction, so she asked, "What, exactly, was it that struck you so funny?"

"It's that I said I only saw you as a child, when in fact, that's exactly what you were!" Once again, he put his arms around her, but this time he pulled her close and kissed her, long and sensuously. Then he pulled away and said, "But not anymore." And she knew—could feel—that not only was she getting a decent man, but also one who was going to provide genuine love, along with interspersed frivolity, for the rest of their days together.

A HOME IN GULLIVER

Two inland lakes, Gulliver Lake to the west of the town and McDonald Lake to the east, were both perfect for gathering loads of ice to suffice the needs of Emmo's customers. In addition, but only when necessary, some of the ice he and his crew collected came from Seul Choix Bay (pronounced *sis-SHWA*) on Lake Michigan's northern shore. The point of land that protected the bay had been named by the French and means "only choice" since it was the sole point of protection for the canoes of Native Americans and French fur traders caught on the open waters of Lake Michigan when an unanticipated storm arose while paddling to or from the Straits of Mackinac sixty miles to the east.

As they approached Gulliver, Rene became aware of the outline of a tower rising above them on the horizon. The daylight was fading, and a lighthouse lamp was casting its beacon in an arc that lit up the twilight sky over the water along the shoreline of the upper peninsula's southern coast. She had never been that far south, as her ma and pop had taken her no farther than Munising to the west, Whitefish Point to the east, and Seney to the south. Between 1892 and 1895 the Seul Choix lighthouse had been built on Seul Choix Pointe which, throughout the mid-1800s, had supported a thriving Native American fishing community. The tower light shone from eighty feet above the water level of Lake Michigan and operated a fog signal in the form of a ten-inch steam whistle, though Rene would not hear that sound for almost a week, as the skies would remain clear for the next few days and nights.

Stars had already begun to appear where it was darkest overhead; no moon was to be seen. "I had no idea we'd be living where I can see a light," she said to Emmo, excitement in her voice. "I'll feel right at home, except the inner and outer range lights in Grand Marais aren't nearly so tall or impressive."

Emmo had stopped the wagon. When she looked around, they were sitting in front of a stone cottage, the likes of which she had never encountered. Inside a stone wall that encircled the property, Rene could make out impressive landscaping—trees and shrubs and flower beds overflowing with fall blooms. In the twilight she could see redwood shutters at each window of the house, and a half-hipped roof made the place look like it came straight out of *Hansel and Gretel* or *Snow White*. A double-doored stable was located not more than 60 feet from the house with a cobblestone walkway that disappeared behind the cottage. Another cobblestone walk, but wider, curved from the drive to an inviting stoop and a round-topped wooden front door.

"Oh, Emmo! This is your house? This is where you live?"

He smiled and nodded.

"Oh, my! Oh, my!" She had no other words.

He climbed down from the ice wagon. Grog and Ivy started to move toward the stable, not understanding why they had been stopped at the road. Emmo's soft "Whoa, easy," along with his gentle hand on them, calmed them, and they remained standing still, though their nickers and snorts and nodding heads told Rene they wanted desperately to go to the stable for their evening meal of hay and a bit of grain, and for the feel of soft straw beneath their hooves. Unlike her, they were unimpressed with the night sky, the lighthouse, and the cottage.

    Emmo went to her side of the wagon and extended his arms toward her, beckoning her down. She allowed him to lift her from the seat and place her on the ground, the sound of crunching gravel beneath her feet. He put one of his long, strong arms around her shoulders and pulled her close. "Welcome to my home…yours too, for now."

1918

THE SISTERS

"It's always so good to see you alongside Emmo up there on the wagon," Pearl said to Rene as they embraced. Then, arms around one another, they walked through the boarding house lobby and out toward the large back porch that faced the harbor. Pearl had taken over Rene's job when Rene left Grand Marais ten years earlier. In 1912 the boarding house owners had been forced to move to a warmer clime secondary to the husband's debilitating rheumatism. His limbs had become twisted, the joints gnarled and painful, so the doctor in Munising had advised a move southward and/or westward. They had sold the boarding house to Pearl; she was now buying it from them on time, little by little.

Emmo lingered inside long enough to pour a lemonade for each of them. It was a warm Indian-Summer day in late September; stifling, humid air had greeted Emmo and Rene when they rode into town. Rene was surprised to see Pearl's three sisters sitting at a small, round, wrought iron table; all three were fanning themselves with wide paper fans on wooden handles. Ruby and Opal rose and embraced Rene like one of their own. Rene was overcome with emotion at being so lovingly accepted by the two of them. Garnet, the eldest of the four sisters, remained seated and, without changing her sour expression, merely nodded at Rene.

When Ruby and Opal had pulled up chairs for Rene and Emmo, Ruby, bubbling with joy, said to Rene, "If the look on your face is any indication, then you are obviously living a happy life." She patted Rene's hand.

Garnet tilted her head slightly and, without so much as a hint of a smile, asked, in a deep voice, "Emmo treating you well?"

"Better than well, thank you, Garnet."

Emmo appeared at the door, and Ruby rapidly motioned for him to come and sit. Pearl turned back toward the boarding house's lobby, as someone had appeared at the front desk, and it was Pearl's place to address the person's needs. In typical Emmo fashion, he bent down and brushed cheeks with Ruby and Opal. Ruby giggled and blushed. "Garnet," he said, emotionless, as he nodded in her direction.

Emmo and Rene most certainly did have a good life. She accompanied him at least once a month on his delivery route in order to visit the people with whom she'd grown up and to capture a revitalizing dose of Lake Superior and the harbor town that had been her home for 19 years. She and Emmo no longer had the pleasure of anticipating an entertaining evening with Grange Reiker, as the railroad had come to an end along with the logging business in Grand Marais. In 1911 the rails had been taken up and shipped out to Minnesota where they were reassembled for a new line there, and Grange had been shipped out with them.

For nearly an hour, they all chatted amiably, all except Garnet, who appeared to be bored with both the conversation and the company. Rene never once saw her smile, or for that matter, react in any way other than to exhibit mere tolerance. Eventually Emmo put his massive hands on his knees and said, "I must take my leave. I have three more stops to make, and the ice isn't getting any colder sitting in the wagon in this heat." He rose and put a hand on Rene's shoulder. As he turned to leave, she reached up and put her hand on his. They didn't need to exchange words; their touch said it all.

Rene noticed that Garnet turned away, a hint of disgust momentarily crossing her face as she witnessed the touch. "Tell me, Garnet, have you finished that beautiful tablecloth you were crocheting when we were here last?" Rene asked.

Garnet's head swiveled toward Rene as if it had slowly been

moved by the hand of a puppeteer. "And just why would it be of interest to you?"

Opal sighed audibly.

"It seemed such a great undertaking," Rene said. "I can't help but wonder how long such a project takes. I've never practiced the art of crochet."

Ruby was visibly fidgeting and wiggling in her chair. "Garnet loves to crochet, and she's really good at it. I have a bedspread she made for me when I was fifteen, and it has never frayed, even through multiple washings."

Garnet looked at Ruby as if the young woman had spoken out of turn in a stage play, stepping on the star's line. Ruby laced her fingers in her lap and put her head down. One would have thought she was being punished. Garnet turned back to Rene. "I plan to have it finished by Christmas. It seems it's my year to *provide* a dinner for my sisters," she said, putting a great amount of emphasis on the word "provide."

"You are a great cook, Garnet," Pearl said. "And it would be a shame for you to hide such a talent under a bushel basket." Pearl looked expectantly at each of her sisters. "Don't you agree?" She was hoping they would acknowledge the compliment, knowing that compliments were the one thing that could shift Garnet's attitude from sullen to acceptable. But no one spoke, and Garnet's oppressive silence prevailed.

Rene finally piped up, "So...I'm guessing you hope to use the tablecloth for Christmas dinner then."

"Was that not clear?" Garnet asked. There was another long silent pause.

Ruby blurted, "Rene, why don't you and Emmo join us at Garnet's place for Christmas this year?"

Garnet's head snapped toward her youngest sister. Her eyes grew as large as saucers, her lips were pursed causing the spaces between the age lines to turn white. She straightened in her seat so as to gain at least three inches of height, and her fists were clenched on the arms of her chair.

Ruby's face turned ashen. Rene could read Ruby's mind: she was panic-stricken about what Garnet might say or do at that moment, even though the young woman continued to smile. Slowly Ruby turned toward Pearl. In a breathy voice she asked, "What say you, Pearl? Wouldn't it be fun to spend the holiday with Rene and Emmo?"

Pearl appeared unshaken. "I think it's a wonderful idea, Ruby."

"And I agree," said Opal without hesitation.

Rene, unwavering, said, "I'll run it by Emmo. I really would love to see that tablecloth, Garnet." She picked up her glass and drank the last of her lemonade without taking her eyes off Garnet. Rene knew it took everything Pearl, Ruby, and Opal had to keep from snorting; they didn't dare look at one another at that moment.

THANKSGIVING

Indian summer lingered throughout October that year. Even November was warmer than normal, though the temperature dipped below freezing at night on several occasions. On the day before Thanksgiving, Emmo left to make his usual two-day journey to Grand Marais and back. He had shot a grouse the day before, and he and Rene dressed it and put it in the ice box for their Thanksgiving meal.

On the morning of Thanksgiving, Rene got up early and began to prepare their feast. She baked a pumpkin pie using two small pumpkins that had grown in their garden. She baked a loaf of soda bread and kept it wrapped in a towel to keep it warm. Half a jar of apple butter remained in the ice box, so she removed it and set it next to the stove to allow it to reach room temperature (she thought it always had more flavor when it was warm). From the root cellar she gathered a quart of canned snap beans, a bowl of potatoes, an onion, a few carrots, and some rutabagas and turnips. She planned to mash the rutabagas and turnips. She would heat up the beans with some bacon grease and a bit of chopped onion. The grouse would be roasted in the Dutch oven along with the potatoes and carrots, which she would smother with butter, salt, and pepper, and she'd make sop gravy from the drippings.

She sang as she worked; she was happier than she had been in a long time. She couldn't wait for Emmo to get home, not only for the feast, but also because she had a special surprise for him. He arrived around 4:30, whistling as usual. He tended to the horses then headed toward the house. Rene was waiting for him at the back door.

"Happy Thanksgiving!" Rene greeted him with a kiss on the cheek.

Emmo closed his eyes, took a deep breath, and said, "The house smells wonderful!" He looked around and saw the pies, the bread, the pots and pans on the stove, and the holiday table already set. "You've been busy."

"All I have left to do is boil the turnips and rutabagas and mash them, and I have to heat up the snap beans. Oh, and make the gravy."

"What can I do to help?" he asked.

"You can take off that awful-smelling coat and leave it on the porch. It smells like Grog and Ivy." She made an unpleasant face.

"I think I can manage that," he said.

Rene continued to hum as she cooked. Emmo smiled; he appeared to enjoy knowing she was happy. Rene was keenly aware that he sometimes had doubts about their relationship because he was so much older, even though she told him he was silly for thinking such a thing.

They exchanged pleasant conversation during the meal. Emmo told her about his trip and whom he had talked to at his various stops. "Pearl sends her regards," he said. "She has some news." He stuffed another bite of bread with apple butter into his mouth and smiled smugly, not looking up at Rene.

"Well?"

"Well what?" he asked, prolonging the suspense.

"Come on. Out with it!" Rene demanded.

"It's about Ruby."

"Alright. What about Ruby?"

Emmo took another bite but remained silent.

"Maarten Vandersligh!" Emmo jumped and looked up at

her; she seldom used his given name, and when she did, she usually meant business. "Is it good or bad news?" Her patience was growing thinner with each passing second.

"It seems that Ruby has…." Emmo took his time to wipe the corners of his mouth with his napkin.

Rene rolled her eyes.

"…a beau."

"A serious one?"

"Pearl seems to think so."

"Who is it?"

"I don't think you know him."

An exasperated sigh slipped through her lips. "Well, the only way to be sure is if you tell me his name."

He looked up at an angle and frowned. "Now let me think…" He rubbed his chin. "It was something like…maybe Walton…"

"Walters?" she asked excitedly.

"That might be it."

"Jesse Walters' son? Oh, what is his name? It starts with an R…"

"Reese," Emmo said.

"Yes! Reese Walters. Oh, if that doesn't beat all! That boy was a real ruffian when he was young. I hope he's seen the error of his ways. I'd hate to think someone as naïve as Ruby would get herself tied up with the likes of him. Unless he's changed, of course."

Emmo leaned back in his chair and rubbed his belly. "Contentment is the only real wealth,"[1] he said, sighing in what appeared to be pure ecstacy. He used his pinky fingernail to pick his teeth, looked at what he'd extracted, then re-ate whatever morsel it was that he'd retrieved from between two of his molars.

"Oh, for heaven's sake, Emmo. How crass!"

He burst out laughing. "It's just so good, I didn't want any of it to go to waste."

Rene softened. "Well, that's an odd compliment, but I'll take it." They both laughed.

"So tell me more about Reese."

"I have it on the best authority that Reese was just elected sheriff of Schoolcraft County. I guess he left his prior reputation behind him. He's going to be *upholding* the law now instead of *breaking* it, though I'm not sure his previous antics were actually against the law. I think he just hovered around that fine line between legal and illegal but never really crossed it. Anyway, he and Ruby are officially engaged. They wanted to wait until the election was over before they formally announced it. And Pearl was really disappointed that you weren't with me so she could inform you in person."

Rene sat back in her chair and smiled. "I'm so happy for Ruby. For a long time she's been putting up with Garnet's abusive tongue." She shook her head. "Ruby was never able to handle it as well as Pearl or Opal. I think it's because she has such a kind heart. Not that Pearl and Opal don't. I'm only saying that they could overlook Garnet easier than Ruby ever could."

"Why do you suppose that is?" Emmo asked. "Do you think it's because she was the youngest, and Garnet took advantage of that fact?"

"That may have had something to do with it, but I think it's mostly a personality clash between the two of them. And while we're on the subject, why is Garnet so nasty to you? What did you ever do to her to make her so acidic when you're around?"

Emmo looked Rene straight in the eyes and said, "I jilted her."

Rene's mouth dropped open. "I never knew…when did…when were the two of you…?"

"Water under the bridge," Emmo said dispassionately.

Rene's mouth was still gaping.

"It was when you were little, Rene. You had no interest in my love-life at that stage. My interest in women meant nothing to you. You were more interested in trying to knock me off the seat of my wagon with snowballs, just like all the other kids in town."

She closed her mouth and looked away, trying to recall a time when her current husband would have been interested in someone else romantically. She knew he must have had relationships with other women, but the fact that one of them had been Garnet was simply too big a pill to swallow. "Pearl never said anything about it."

"That's because Pearl's a good woman—almost as good as you."

"But she's my best friend," Rene said, still not looking at Emmo. "How could she possibly have kept it a secret?"

"She didn't want to hurt your feelings? Make you think you were second best?"

Rene snapped her head toward Emmo. "Am I?"

"Oh, for heaven's sake, Rene. I didn't mean it that way. I never had romantic feelings for that woman. At that age, she was just a…a drinking buddy. We would occasionally have a beer at *The Sandy Pier* and talk about what was happening in the world. She never meant anything at all to me. She was never the type of woman who would submit to being someone's partner. Garnet was a rough old girl. Always so negative. Everything and everyone she spoke of was wrong. She said nothing good about a single soul, and nothing that took place was any good because it wasn't being done the way she thought it should have been." He paused. "And she doesn't appear to have changed."

"But you said you jilted her. Doesn't that indicate that she had feelings for you?"

Emmo sighed heavily and rubbed his forehead. "I was a dolt at that age, Rene. What she took for my interest in her was completely unfounded, or so I thought. I didn't recognize that I was leading her on. The whole thing was totally unintentional. And when I finally woke up and realized where it was going, I put an end to it."

Rene was silent for a while. Eventually she said, "I'm not accusing you of being insensitive, Emmo. I can't imagine that you ever could be. You are so perceptive to my every mood." She smiled and emitted a slight chortle. "At times, you seem to know what's going on in my head even before I do."

"Garnet bears a grudge for something that was totally baseless from my point of view, be that legitimate or no. At any rate,

I honestly feel no compulsion to make amends for something she saw in a different light. It means nothing to me. *She* means nothing to me. Whatever it is that she feels, *she* has to deal with it."

"Thank you. I appreciate your openness about the whole thing." Rene took Emmo's large hand in both of hers. "You are right. It truly is water under the bridge."

Emmo sighed in relief and asked, "How about some pie?"

Rene snorted. "If you can hold it after the amount of food you've already put away, I'll gladly cut you a piece."

When the meal was over and the dishes were cleared, Rene put on a pot of coffee. She and Emmo planted themselves on the settee and chatted about the general status quo while the coffee boiled. When it was done, she handed a cup to Emmo. "I have a surprise for you."

"It can't be any better than that pie," Emmo said.

She put her hands on her belly.

Emmo's eyes grew large. "Are you…?"

She smiled and nodded.

ROSIE

Two days before Christmas eve, Emmo prepared to leave earlier than usual to make his deliveries. Normally at that time of year, the weather would have been in the freezing zone, enough so for people to keep things cold without having to depend on M.O. Vandersligh's ice. But a mild fall had lingered, and on that particular day, the thermometer wouldn't dip below 40 degrees.

At 3:30 a.m. Emmo was already loaded up and ready to leave. He told Rene, "There are a lot of people who need a lot of ice for the holidays, so I'll be making some extra stops with a chock-full-to-the-brim wagon. I need to get going."

"I understand," Rene assured him, yawning. "Just be extra careful. It's hard to see the ruts in the road before the sun comes up."

"That's Grog and Ivy's job," he said, snickering.

"I'm serious, Emmo."

"I know you are, and I love you all the more for it." He

grabbed his gloves and his tuque. He still had as much hair as when they had gotten married, though it was nearly white, and his beard matched. He was 57 years old. It was unheard of for a hard-working man to live so long, and even more unusual for one to continue working as hard as Emmo did. But he always said, "It is no achievement to walk a tightrope laid flat on the floor. Where there is no risk, there can be no pride in achievement and, consequently, no happiness."[2] He gave Rene a peck on the cheek, patted her belly, and took his leave, whistling all the way to the stable.

Her pregnancy wasn't really showing yet; she would only be at twelve weeks on Christmas day. They had decided to go to Garnet's house, as Ruby had suggested. Rene had some reservations, especially since they planned to tell all of them about the baby that was on the way. She knew it would be hard on Garnet, but the fact that Garnet's three other sisters would be thrilled overrode her hesitation. She had expressed her feelings to Emmo, but he said, "Garnet be damned!" and she figured, *How can I argue with that?* In fact, Rene was actually eager to spill the beans.

She didn't go back to bed that morning. Instead, she gathered up all the dirty clothes and sorted them into piles of like colors. Then she stripped the bed. She went to the pump on the end of the sink and filled three large kettles which she would heat over the fire. She'd do the washing when daylight arrived. As usual, she hummed as she worked, a habit she had inherited from her ma.

While the water was on its way to boiling, she took off her nightgown, throwing it onto the pile of whites, and got dressed in her day clothes. The sun was rising and sharing its light, so Rene sat down with a counted cross-stitch sampler she needed to finish for Pearl before they left for Grand Marais on Christmas morning. She had done one for each of the sisters, but Pearl's was more involved than the other three; she wasn't concerned about them feeling slighted at its obviously more detailed pattern, because Pearl was her best friend, and a bit more effort on her sampler was to be expected.

After about fifteen minutes, she rose to check the temperature of the water, but a pain in her belly made her gasp. She clutched her lower abdomen and willed herself to breathe. She took in small breaths at first, increasing the amount of air she could tolerate as the next few minutes passed. Finally, she was able to stand up straight. Her heart, however, was racing. Having had no previous experience with pregnancy, either her own or anyone close to her, she was uncertain as to whether the incident had something to do with the baby or if it was simply secondary to something she had eaten the night before.

She sat back down and put her head on the back of the chair, still breathing as calmly as she could. She could see steam rising from the kettle that was closest to the coals. She stood up, gingerly at first, then with more direction. Her heartrate was nearing normal. But as she reached out toward the hook on which the steaming kettle hung, another pain sliced through her body, and she began to sweat.

She was just able to pull the hook toward her, moving the kettle far enough away from the fire to avoid the risk of it eventually boiling dry and cracking. *Oh, Emmo, of all the days to leave so early, why did it have to be today.* She felt her belly tightening up again. She clenched her teeth and sucked in air, but the pain was bad enough to make her cry out. She waited until it subsided, then she grabbed the coffee pot and used it to dip water from the large kettle and pour it over the existing fire—something she would never do under normal circumstances. Those coals were precious, and she knew it would take a long time and a lot of wood to build up new ones, but she also knew she was going to have to leave the house and couldn't allow the fire to burn. And she was in too much pain to bank the coals.

Leland Robeson was Emmo's righthand man. His wife, Rosie, was a Chippewa medicine woman. She was familiar with every plant in the area and what it could do *to* or *for* someone. She was also the local midwife. And somehow Rene knew she needed Rosie's help. It would take every bit of strength she had to walk the half-mile south toward their house, which stood closer to the Seul Choix light.

Another pain drove Rene to her knees, but it passed as she

knelt there, coffee pot in hand. She closed her eyes and prayed for enough stamina to make it to Rosie's without passing out on the side of the road. Eventually she was able to stand, and she forced herself to put on her coat, hat, and gloves. Then she went to the door, opened it, and stepped outside.

A strong, biting wind hit her in the face, and she turned her head and put her hand up to block it. She took one step, then another, then another, and before long, she was walking. The air crept under her coat, and she was aware of dampness on her legs. Something inside her told her it was blood. *I have to keep moving. I can't stop. Keep walking. Walk, Rene. Walk.*

The road seemed longer than it ever had. She was aware of every inch that passed under her feet. Another pain, but she forced herself to keep moving in spite of it. She didn't know if she had screamed; she only knew she wanted to. Her foot caught on a rock, and she stumbled. Everything slowed to a snail's pace. She reached out as if there were something to grab hold of, something to keep her from falling. She looked up at the early dawn and saw the lighthouse's bright arc flash overhead. *What is happening to me? I've never had this kind of pain. I think I'm going to die.* "Emmo? Oh, Emmo, come for me. Help me," she half-whispered, half-spoke.

"I am not Emmo, but I am here to help," a woman's voice said, and a warm hand took the hand with which Rene had reached out. The woman's other arm went around Rene's waist and guided her to the side of the road where there was a large rock, and she sat Rene down on it. Rene looked up into the woman's eyes; they belonged to Rosie.

"How did you find me?" Rene asked.

"Now is not the time for talk," Rosie said. She handed Rene something to drink. It tasted the way rose petals smell, and Rene drank it all, enjoying the way it felt in her mouth and sliding down her throat. Then Rosie walked away for a moment, but she returned with a travois that was padded with pine boughs and covered with a blanket. Rene allowed Rosie to lead her to the travois and lay her down on it. Rosie began to sing in her own language, low at first, then louder and louder as she strapped the contraption around herself and lifted two straps with a fur-covered strip that she put over her head and rested on her forehead. As she began to move forward, Rene could feel herself being towed along, away from her home, toward Seul Choix Bay.

She awakened to the aromas of sweet grass and blueberries. She looked around and realized she was in a strange room, a tiny room with no windows, but she knew, somehow, that it was daylight. At the doorway was a curtain made of a thin material, like gauze, that allowed light to pass through, but she could not see what was on the other side. She closed her eyes for a moment, then she reopened them to make sure she was not dreaming. The vision remained.

Rosie pulled the curtain aside and came into the room, stepping up beside the bed and looking down at Rene. "You need to sleep longer. But you will only sleep for one, now."

Rene blinked a few times, swallowed, then, quite matter-of-factly, said, "I lost the baby."

Rosie gave her a single nod.

"Back there…on the road…how did you find me?"

"I knew you would be there," Rosie said. Then she turned and left.

Rene slept again. At some point she called for Rosie, but there was no answer. She assumed the woman was outside doing chores, so she managed to get up out of bed and use the chamber pot Rosie had left for her. She slid it under the bed when she finished, promising herself she would clean it later.

She slept again, though she did not know for how long. When she opened her eyes, the dim light of evening was making the windowless room darker than it had been when she had gone to sleep. Emmo was sitting beside her. She reached for him, and he took her hand. "Merry Christmas," he said in a low, soft voice.

Unable to speak aloud, she whispered, "Christmas? Is today Christmas?"

He smiled. "Almost. It's Christmas Eve."

Rene looked into his eyes, and he smiled the most loving smile she had ever seen. She sat up, and Emmo helped her scoot back on the mattress and lean against the wall. She whispered again, "We're supposed to go to Garnet's tomorrow."

Emmo shook his head. "I sent a telegram to let them know we won't be there."

Her eyes got big and her brow furrowed. "Did you tell them why?"

"I only said you were ill and could not make the trip," Emmo said.

Rene sighed and relaxed. "Thank you for your discretion."

There was a soft knock on the wooden frame of the curtained doorway. "Come in," Rene said, her voice now thick and scratchy. Rosie entered. She had laundered Rene's dress and undergarments and spot-cleaned the blood that had found its way onto Rene's coat. She placed them on a trunk at the foot of the bed, then she turned and left. Within a few seconds, she returned with a tray holding a bowl of broth, a cup of tea, and a small glass filled with a foggy mixture.

"Drink the liquid from the small glass first; it does not taste good, but it will keep you from bleeding. Then you may finish the broth and tea. Emmo will bring the wagon for you tomorrow." She left them alone.

Emmo and Rene looked at each other. Rene whispered, "But I want to go home today. Can't you talk to her and…"

"I've already talked to her, and she will not allow me to take you yet. She says I can come back to get you first thing in the morning."

"I guess you'll be my Christmas present, huh?"

He nodded ever so slightly. "I know having you home will be the best Christmas present I ever got."

1926

BAD WEATHER'S CURSE

Rosie had told Rene, "Do not allow yourself to be with child again." Rene and Emmo had heeded the wise woman's words.

It was early May, and Emmo was preparing to make his final ice delivery. He was retiring and was in the process of selling the business to Leland. Rene had mixed emotions about getting rid of the ice business, but Emmo told her, "We cannot avoid meeting great issues. All that we can determine for ourselves is whether we shall meet them well or ill."[3] They had plenty of money to last them throughout their lives, so they were not concerned that the sale price would not bring in what the business was potentially worth. Instead, they were delighted that Leland was able to come up with enough to make him feel good about the deal.

Refrigeration was on the horizon, so Leland had been busy talking to various company representatives who could ship the ice in refrigerated train cars to places where the railroad was available. It would mean a large increase in income for Leland and Rosie. Leland would need to find someone to take over the part of Emmo's delivery route that ran between Seney and Grand Marais, however, since those rail lines had been removed.

The weather that day was iffy, at best. There were dark clouds to the north, and a harsh wind was disturbing last fall's leaves, the ones that always lingered on the ground under the snow till spring temperatures uncovered them enough that they could be blown around. "Are you sure you're dressed warm enough for this weather?" Rene asked.

"As sure as a man can be," Emmo said.

She sighed. "Sometimes you seem to take things too lightly. From the looks of the northern sky, this could turn into something quite nasty before you get back home tomorrow."

"Worry wart," he said and playfully smacked her backside as he passed her on the way to the door.

She turned as if to smack him back, but instead, she grabbed him by the lapels of his coat and kissed him full on the lips.

It took Emmo by surprise. "What brought that on?"

"I just want to send you off on your last trip with something that'll make you want to come back home to me."

"Well...if I *have* to," he teased. Grinning, he touched her cheek tenderly and left.

The weather did not improve. It was damp and cold, and before noon, it started to rain—that awful rain that runs down the inside of your collar and soaks right through your clothes. The kind of rain that's half-frozen and pelts you as if each drop has a personal vendetta to settle.

Rene was glad she had decided not to go with Emmo on this trip. She knew he'd spend more time at each stop because everyone would be giving him their regards on his retirement, and she'd likely be sitting on the wagon seat getting colder and wetter by the minute which would, in turn, cause her to be less than jovial. An involuntary shiver overtook her, and she wrapped her arms around herself. She knew the bed would be chilly tonight without Emmo there to keep her warm. She was thankful he'd be comfortably warm at Pearl's boarding house.

That night and the whole next day the miserable weather continued. Emmo didn't arrive home until after dark. He unhitched the horses and followed them into the stable where he tended to their stalls and their feed, but he didn't take time to clean out the wagon. There would be lots of wet straw that would soon make the inside of the wagon smell bad. She frowned. *That's unlike him.*

He came in without stopping to say hello and walked straight to the fireplace. She noticed him shivering, and as she came closer, she could hear a rattle when he breathed. "Can I bother you for a cup of hot coffee?" he asked, coughing. His voice was scratchy and nearly two octaves lower than usual, and his words broke up as he spoke.

"Of course. That's a good idea." she said. She ran water into the coffee pot from the pump on the sink. "You sound terrible."

"Don't feel any better than I sound, either." He coughed again, a deep, unforgiving cough.

"This weather's to blame," Rene said. "I knew it was bad, and I hated to see you leave. I felt like you were disappearing into some dark abyss as you rode out of sight yesterday morning." She added coffee grounds to the ones already in the pot, threw in some crushed eggshells to make the grounds settle, and set it on the stove. She lit the burner and said, "It shouldn't take too long. I only put about half the water in that I normally do, so it'll boil quicker. I can always make more if you want it."

Emmo shed his wet coat and hat as he stood there in front of the blaze. He added more wood, and the flame rose. He was breathing through his mouth, struggling to get air into his lungs.

Rene grabbed the quilt off their bed and started toward him. "You need to get out of those wet clothes, too," she said. "I'll stand here and get the quilt warm for when you come back."

He said nothing as he passed her. When he returned, he had changed into a dry pair of long underwear and heavy wool socks. He grabbed the quilt and folded it around himself, closing his eyes and coughing. Rene pulled a chair up to the fireplace. He took it from her and sat down as close to the fire as he could without the danger of igniting. He raised the quilt up over his face and coughed again. "I got so chilled," he growled. "Glad you decided not to go." The mere act of speaking caused him to cough more.

She was going to ask after Pearl but decided against it. She perched on the edge of the settee and refrained from talking. Emmo's breathing was uneven and more pronounced in the silence. It worried her. Finally, she said, "I think you should see a doctor tomorrow."

"I will, if I make it through the night." He tried to laugh, but that only caused his coughing to increase. "I'll just stay here by the fire tonight. I have to warm up somehow. I don't remember ever being so cold."

"You probably have a fever," Rene said. She rose and went to him, putting the back of her hand on his forehead. "You're burning up!"

"How can that be when I feel like I'm freezing to death?"

"That's just the way fevers are. Have you never had one before?" she asked, unable to grasp the concept of someone not knowing what a fever felt like.

"Maybe once. As a kid. Not since."

She moved the chair he'd been sitting in and pulled the settee over closer to the fireplace, making him curl up on it. Then she went to the kitchen and ran a couple of dish cloths under the cold water of the pump. She took them in and put one on Emmo's forehead. He jumped, but then he settled down and said, "Feels pretty good even though I'm cold inside." More coughing. "My head's thumping like a rabbit's foot. Is the coffee ready yet?" He barely finished the question before going into a full-fledged coughing fit. He covered his mouth with the quilt as he coughed, and Rene could see traces of blood at the site.

"I'll bring you some as soon as it finishes boiling." She went back into the kitchen. With shaking hands, she took a cup down from the cupboard and put a bit of milk and a teaspoon of honey into it. Then she picked up the coffee pot with a corner of her apron, which she wadded into a bunch, and poured the hot, black brew over the milk and honey. It smelled divine, and she thought seriously about pouring a cup for herself after she took Emmo's cup to him. But he was already asleep, rattling and rasping with each breath and shivering every few seconds. She didn't wake him; she thought it best to let him sleep.

She gathered up two more blankets and covered him, hoping he'd sweat out the fever. She could remember, as a child, how good it felt when a fever would break. She hoped the same would happen for Emmo. She drank the coffee, mostly to keep herself awake, and spent the next few hours tending the fire and changing the cool cloths on Emmo's forehead. By midnight, he had stopped shivering, but he was still feverish, and the sounds in his chest were getting worse.

As soon as daylight appeared, Rene walked to Leland and Rosie's house. The native woman wasted no time gathering up all manner of baskets and jars of God-knew-what, then she opened the door and headed toward Rene and Emmo's place. It took every bit of energy Rene had to keep up with the woman. In no time, they were at the door of the stone cottage, and Rosie didn't wait to be invited in; she opened the door and barreled into the living room where Emmo was still curled up on the settee.

Rosie closed her eyes and listened to his breathing. Then she knelt down and put her ear to his chest. She sat back on her feet and began to chant. She opened several of the baskets and jars and said to Rene, "I need to make tea. Boil water." It was a demand, not a request. Rene was scared and immediately did as she had been told.

For nearly an hour Rosie worked her magic on Emmo. Rene did her best to stay out of the way but remained available in case Rosie needed something. Rene was so tired she could hardly hold her eyes open. Then Rosie's hand was on her shoulder, and she realized she had dozed off sitting at the table. "Is there any change?" she asked, looking up at Rosie.

Rosie stared down at her without responding to the question. Rene stood up as if she had been catapulted from the chair and looked into Rosie's eyes. The answer was there. Emmo was gone.

1927

A NEW HOME

Rene listed the stone cottage with a real estate company in Manistique. The agency assured her the place would sell quickly, and she was certain they were right. She was going back to Grand Marais; Lake Superior was calling. She knew her old house might not be salvageable, but she would tear it down and rebuild, if need be. In the meantime, she would stay at Pearl's house. Rene had offered to pay for a room at the boarding house, but Pearl had insisted on keeping Rene at her home, saying, "That's what best friends are for." And Rene had finally agreed.

It was the second week of June when she rode into Grand Marais. Leland drove her there, dropped her off at Pearl's, and promised that he and Rosie would keep in touch. As he drove away, Rene closed her eyes and took a deep breath, filling her lungs with the scent of Lake Superior, her lake. The temperature was balmy, the sky azure, and the nearly-ever-present wind was driving three-foot swells onto Grand Marais's shoreline. *It truly is my home*, she thought. *As much as I loved being with Emmo at the stone cottage, it never felt like this. This is where I belong. Lucky are the few who know the satisfaction of finding that one special place on this earth that cannot be separated from the heart. Far more than a mere feeling, it's a concreteness that clings to the soul. Coming home to that special place revitalizes and reconditions every bone and muscle in the body.*

The next morning Rene stood on the road in front of her old house, which had become an eyesore. She knew it would require extensive repairs and updates, both outside and in, if she chose to leave it standing. *It's only wood and nails*, she thought. *It's not some keepsake that I can display on a shelf. It's a house, and houses are being built with insulated walls now, and oil heaters, and electric lights, and indoor toilets. Why not start over, from the ground up? It doesn't need to be large. Maybe it can sit on the same foundation.* But after closer examination, she realized the foundation, too, was cracked and broken in spots and would have to be replaced as well. But that piece of land was home, and that's where she would live. For a brief moment, sad memories overtook her, and she couldn't remember feeling so downhearted, so morose, so alone. She cried—a long, hard cry—hoping some of the sorrow she'd been feeling would evaporate along with her tears.

Emmo had left everything to her, and that amounted to quite a sum of money, not including the profits yet to come from the sale of the stone cottage in Gulliver. She thought, *Living by myself shouldn't frighten me. I should be able to accept it just as I accepted being alone following the deaths of Ma and Pop and Emmo and our child. I'll always miss them, but I've more than proven my ability to overcome such losses.* Even so, in some remote corner of her mind—a place she couldn't put her finger on—there was a dark, agonizing, unpleasantness that occasionally reared its ugly head.

The maple tree that her ma and pop had planted only ten feet away from the end of the house was now draped over and around the decaying building, cradling it so that only a small portion of the house was disclosed. The roof sagged in the middle and displayed obvious holes. *The inside must be completely destroyed, having been exposed to the weather for so many years.* The large, flat stones that created a stoop had settled and pulled away from the threshold. She carefully stepped up to the door, the bottom of which was rotted away so that a few pieces of it hung loosely dangling above the threshold. *I wonder how many animals have made their homes inside.*

She pushed on the door using both hands, and it gave way, part of it crumbling into pieces at her touch and part clinging to the rusty, decomposing hinges. The smells were overpowering: mildew, mold, animal odors, dampness, rotting wood. She took three steps into the room, but she was afraid to go any farther, thinking she might fall through the flooring, or that the whole house might come tumbling down on her. She heard a rustling noise overhead. *Squirrels? Birds? Racoons? Pine martens?* She remained stark still, listening, and the sound moved from one end of the attic to the other, toward the big maple tree. *Something has found a way in by climbing up that tree.*

She retraced her steps, exiting the house by stepping backwards in her own footprints that were evident in the dirt on the floor. *It held me up once; it should tolerate my weight again*, she hoped. When she reached the door, she looked up at the ceiling. In the darkness it appeared to be intact, though she had no idea how that could have been possible. She could only make out a couple of water stains on the floor in the main room, but she was sure there had to be others. She'd need more light to be certain.

Making her way back to the road, she knew it would be ridiculously naïve to think she could save what was left of the place. She turned to look at it once again, and her peripheral vision caught something moving away from her at the base of the big maple. *That settles it*, she thought. *I'm going to have the place flattened. I should have done it years ago. And I'm sure everyone in town feels that way, too.* She could feel herself blushing from embarrassment, her cheeks and neck becoming warm. Then she remembered something Grange told her once: "The most difficult thing is the decision to act. The rest is merely tenacity."[3]

She walked back to Pearl's house. She needed to take some time to think things through, knowing she would have to find someone who could tear down the old house and take away the rubble. Then she would need to find a builder and a stone mason. She wanted the lower part of the house to be river stone, like Emmo's, and the upper portion to be made of logs. She wasn't sure about the roof, so she'd talk to the builder about it, hoping his advice was sound. She also knew she wanted a house that was built for two people. *I'm still young enough to get married again if the right person comes along.*

She would be able to afford to pay cash for the work; it was only a matter of withdrawing it from the bank. But she wanted to make sure she didn't use up too much of it all at once, considering she would have to live off that money for the rest of her life. So she would make an appointment with someone at the bank to discuss various ways of making her savings grow. As she pondered all the possibilities, she realized she was smiling; she couldn't remember having done that for quite some time.

ALVIE WYBEL

"Please be careful of the tree," Rene said to Nels, the elderly man who was dismantling the old house. He was working on the west side where the big maple tree grew. "I want to keep it."

Nels lifted his face toward the top of the huge maple. "Wit a bit of trimmin', it'll give ya some nice shade on da days when da heat rises and da wind don't blow, eh? I'll be mindful of it, doncha know." He continued removing the siding and tossing the boards onto a pile. The uprights that supported the roof appeared to be rotted, and Rene worried that they would collapse and the remains would come crashing down on the man. But Nels was the expert, so she felt she owed it to him to trust his judgment.

She had walked down from Pearl's place to the property at about four that afternoon, just to make her presence known. About twenty minutes passed; she had spent the time looking around the property, and Nels continued tearing the exterior boards off the house. It was evident that he had spent most of the day removing the large rocks that had once been the front stoop and had only started on the siding shortly before she'd arrived. He came to an abrupt halt and backed away from his work. "Missus Vandersligh," he said softly, "der seems ta be sometin in yer attic."

"I thought I heard something a few days ago. I couldn't make out what animal it might have been."

"But animals…" he shook his head, "…dey don't have footsteps dat sound like people's shoes crossin' da floor, eh?" He looked at her, and worry lines creased his forehead.

She stepped closer to the house, or what was left of it, and turned her head, cupping her hand behind her right ear. "I don't hear anything."

Nels did the same, and he, too, admitted there was nothing

audible. He chuckled nervously. "Guess I was just hearin' tings." He had no more than completed the words when a large portion of the roof caved in, smashing down onto the floor of the main room of the house. Both he and Rene jumped, turning their backs to it and covering their heads.

Then all was quiet. Somehow the debris had been contained within the confines of the walls. Rene realized Nels's face was white as a sheet, and beads of sweat had broken out on his forehead.

"It's nearly five o'clock," she said to him. "Why don't you call it a day?"

"Tank you. I tink I will." He smiled sheepishly then hurriedly gathered up his tools, which he haphazardly threw into the bed of his relatively new truck, climbed in behind the steering wheel, and barreled off. Rene hoped he'd return to finish the job.

She turned back toward the pile of remnants that used to be her house. Her mouth dropped open. A boy was standing amidst the rubble that had collapsed into the room. "Hey!" she called. "You mustn't play there. It's very dangerous." But the child merely looked at her and smiled.

"Did you hear me?" She repeated her prior warning.

"I heard you," the boy said, unmoved.

Rene looked down at the ground long enough to find her footing and took a step toward the house, but she ran smack dab into the boy, who had mysteriously and silently appeared right before her. "How did you...?" She raised her head and looked toward the house, fully expecting to see the original boy standing there in what was left of the roof. But no other boy was visible. The boy who had been standing in front of her was now sitting on the ground at her feet. "Weren't you just...?" she pointed toward the house.

"Yeah," the boy said.

"But you couldn't have..."

"Wanna see me do it again?" he asked.

Rene blinked and shook her head to try and clear out the cobwebs that she felt were obviously interfering with her vision, as well as her ability to interpret the scenario that had taken place a few seconds earlier.

"I've been living there for a while," he said, as if it were perfectly normal and to be expected.

"Who are you? And why have you been living in my attic?"

"Alvie Wybel," he said and extended his hand up to her as if expecting a handshake.

"Alvie…"

"Wybel. Alvie Wybel."

Rene's mouth hung open, and she looked from Alvie to the house and back again a couple of times, total confusion encompassing her face. She extended her hand down toward the boy's hand and shook it, partly to convince herself that he was a real, solid entity.

"Whew! I'm glad that's over," Alvie said, fiddling with a blade of grass. "The introduction's usually the worst part."

"W…Worst part of what?"

As if she should have known what he meant, he said, shrugging, "Meeting my newest subject."

Again, Rene blinked, her mouth still agape. Eventually her chin came up and her lips met, but she continued to stare at him.

"I know, I know. I should probably be more empathetic, but it's something I've never quite been able to overcome. I still get a kick out of surprising my subjects every time." He giggled.

"So, I'm your newest subject?"

"Yep."

Rene was decidedly confused. "I'm not sure I understand what you mean by 'subject.'"

Surprisingly, Alvie tilted his head ever so slightly and smiled the most touching smile Rene had ever encountered on anyone's face. "I know you've been through a lot, and you have lots of questions like, 'Why did all of those bad things happen to me?' 'How am I gonna get through this alone?' And so on, and so on… So I'm here to help you over the humps."

She whirled around, turning her back to Alvie. She took a deep breath, let it out, and slowly turned to where she had seen what she knew had to be a mere apparition of a young boy sitting before her. Alvie—in the flesh—was still there, smiling up at her, his head still tilted slightly to one side. "Are you my conscience?" she asked him.

"No. We aren't your conscience, but we are a collective consciousness. Every person who's ever existed has had a conscience, which is supposed to help make them know what's right and what's not. Although, unfortunately, not everyone knows how to access it and turn it on." He stood and looked up at her. "I'm not conjured up either; I'm actually real, but I exist on a different plane, one that only *you* can access at any given time. Oh," he said as an afterthought, "and no one else can see or hear me, so when we talk, you'll need to be careful, 'cause if someone's watching, they'll consider having you committed to the loony bin."

"What do you mean *we*? There are more of you?" She allowed her eyes to rove a bit.

"Oh yeah! Gazillions of us. We've existed for eons—since time began, actually. And what you call the Big Bang—well, you won't believe what REALLY happened."

"The big…what?"

He put a finger over his upper lip and appeared to be thinking for a moment. "Oh yeah. Got ahead of myself there." He waved his hand rapidly and said, "Nevermind."

Rene's head was swimming. There had to be a reason why this…this…child was supposed to help her cope with what had been going on in her head, though she had spoken of the matters to no one. "Were you sent here by God?"

Alvie had moved to the stack of siding boards Nels had removed from the end of the house and was picking through them for…well, Rene didn't know for what. "We aren't sent by any deity, not your god or anyone else's. Did you ever think about all the civilizations that have had *multiple* gods: Greeks, Romans, Norsemen—they're the ones you call Vikings—most of the tribes in Africa, Native Americans…" He stopped studying the lumber and looked at her. "And they all had their own gods, and every one of them thought theirs were the only ones. At least the Native Americans talk to the earth, sky, water…but that tobacco thing cracks me up. Almost as good as grape juice and wafers.

Whose idea was that?" Alvie doubled over laughing.

"So, you're like my guardian angel, then?"

Alvie sighed. "We're not guardian angles. We don't *guard* you; we *guide* you. And we are NOT angels," he said, rolling his eyes. "I hate to dispel one of your most precious beliefs, but angels are nothing more than us taking that form so we can gain your trust. Actually, it's not a bad gig. I mean, the whole idea of not having to come up with clothes of the period makes our lives much easier. With angels, you wrap a piece of cloth around your mid-section, drape it over one shoulder, light up a ring around your head, and you're a shoe-in."

"How old are you, Alvie?"

"You mean how old do I appear to you?"

"Okay."

"Nine."

Rene's mouth came open again.

"Actually, I'm ageless. I don't have a birth date. I've been around since before the earth was able to support life. But to you, I'm nine."

"Why that particular age?"

Alvie looked down at the ground for a moment, then he looked back at Rene. He waited until her eyes met his, and he said, "That's how old your son would have been."

"My son? But I don't have any ch…" She stopped, thought a moment, and finally asked, "The baby I lost was a boy?"

He nodded, his eyes not wavering from her gaze.

Barely audible, she said, "I never thought to ask Rosie about it."

"Wouldn't have mattered. She would've said she wasn't able to tell."

Rene had often dreamt about raising their child, and for some reason, it had always been a boy in her dreams. She saw Emmo and the boy going off on fishing trips, getting ready for deer or grouse hunting, tending to the horses together. She saw the boy heading off to school or saw the expressions on his face when listening to her as she read to him from a storybook. She could see them all sitting at the supper table, discussing their day and laughing. Those dreams were always happy, but then she'd awaken, and the realization of their child's absence came down on her. Hard. Then she'd think of Emmo and how desperately she missed him. But her mood would lighten when she allowed her memories to lead her home to Grand Marais and her Great Lake.

HELP FROM A NINE-YEAR-OLD?

Days turned into weeks, and the work on Rene's new house continued. Many of the townspeople remarked about its attractiveness. Rene was excited about it, but she couldn't seem to keep her mind channeled on any one thing. Her thoughts bounced around "like a flea in a hot skillet," as her ma used to say.

Her relationship with Alvie grew by leaps and bounds; he was such an interesting character. "Where do you go when you disappear?" she asked him one evening when she was eating her supper. Alvie didn't eat, but he did enjoy the aromas of certain foods and would wave the scent toward his nose, close his eyes, and inhale deeply. He had let her in on a secret: his favorite was popcorn.

"You aren't my only subject," he said. "I'm also seeing a man in India called a mahatma, which means 'great soul,' a young man here in the United States who will become the president one day—you'll still be around when that happens—and a Negro woman who has much to say about human rights but struggles with non-acceptance from the outside world, even her own race and her own family. But, luckily, she's a journalist, a playwright, and a poet, so she has the potential to be able to express herself in spite of her oppressors. I also see subjects in other timeframes, other universes, and other dimensions."

"How can you manage to be so many places all at once?" Rene asked.

Alvie shook his head. "That's the one thing we can't do; we can't be two places at the same time. We can jump from one timeframe to another, we can change our age, sex, and appearance, and we can go back and forth through countless dimensions and universes, but we can't guide more than one person at any one given moment."

"No wonder there are so many of you."

"Wow! You actually get it!" Alvie was obviously elated at her ability to understand. "On your wedding day, on the way to Emmo's place, he said to you, 'You're a smart woman, Rene Vendersligh.' He was absolutely right."

Rene blushed and changed the subject. "Is it difficult for you to represent yourself as a nine-year-old boy?" she asked. "Because I'd be perfectly happy to share my thoughts and feelings with you if you existed in another form for me."

Alvie gave her that special smile of his. "No difficulty whatsoever—except for the clothes. If I had better fashion sense it'd be easier. But considering that's the toughest thing I have to overcome, I'll live with it. Besides, I like being a nine-year-old boy for you. It makes perfect sense."

Rene simply took him at his word. Then she thought, *I wonder if I would be so understanding if he were older.*

"Nah. You'd probably feel like you'd need to defend your opinion if I were older," Alvie said.

"You just read my thoughts!" Rene said, surprised.

"I've been doing that all along. Most of the time, though, it's better for you to hear both me and yourself say things out loud. Humans are just like that, and I think it's one of the things I like best about them."

"Are there other people…other humans…out there?" She pointed to the sky.

"Yes, there are—well, not humans, exactly, but other similar lifeforms. I just came from a planet where they don't exactly look like humans, but they do walk upright on two legs. And they tend to think along the same lines as humans." He went on to tell her about the vast differences among the subjects he guides and about the abundance of problems they encounter based on their environments and their relationships.

Rene said, "That means you have to understand the entire store of social actions in every situation you encounter. I can't imagine having that horrible burden on my shoulders."

"It's not a burden," he said quietly. "It's an honor."

Rene gasped. "I just insulted you, didn't I? I'm so sorry. I spoke without thinking. I made your whole purpose sound unimaginable, yet here you are with me, a minute speck on…on a vast…photograph of existence. My perception of you must seem…"

He cut her off. "Irene!"

That's exactly how Emmo used to bring me back to reality.

"I know," he said, nodding. "You have to remember: 'perception isn't reality.'[4]" His voice was soothing and childlike. "Think about it: 'even salt and sugar look alike.'[5]"

She paused. "You have the most marvelous way of making me see the truth in things. I never thought about separating reality and perception, though I'm fully aware that they're not the same."

"Aaa, don't beat yourself up about it. A very intelligent man, who's one of your contemporaries, either *has* said or *will* say, "Reality is merely an illusion, albeit a very persistent one."[6]

Rene smiled, and Alvie giggled, reaching up and patting her on the arm.

A very calming action coming from a nine-year-old, she thought and heaved a contented sigh.

Alvie looked up at her and smiled.

1928

THE BREAKTHROUGH

"Oolanaloo," Alvie said.

"Oola...what?"

"Oo-lah-NAH-loo. It's a name that means respect, trust, reverence, independence, oneness."

"What language is that?" Rene asked.

Alvie paused. Then he sighed and looked up at the sky, as if searching for something. "It's not a language you'd be familiar with. I don't mean to belittle your ability to understand, but it would take a whole lot of explaining, and as a human, the result probably wouldn't be within your realm of understanding."

Rene had never been one to turn down the opportunity to prove someone wrong. She said, "Try me."

Again, Alvie paused. "'Beware lest you lose the substance by grasping at the shadow.'"

"You think I'll become so engrossed in trying to figure out the source, I won't see the real gist of the meaning."

"Something like that. What's important is not where it comes from but where it leads. Let me spell Oolanaloo for you, and you tell me what's significant about it. Now close your eyes."

Rene did as Alvie requested.

He spelled slowly, "O-o-l-a-n-a-l-o-o."

Rene could see the word in her mind. "It's a palindrome, spelled the same forwards and backwards, if that's what you're getting at."

"That's exactly what I'm getting at!" Alvie said. He tilted his head and looked at Rene as if he'd never really seen her before.

"And why is that so significant?" she asked.

"Because that's exactly what Oolanaloo is: the same forwards and backwards."

"Is Oolanaloo a he or a she? Or an it?"

Alvie shook his head. "None of the above. Oolanaloo *is*."

"Is what?" she asked.

"Just…*is*."

She thought about that for several beats, then she said, "I think I understand. There's no place where Oolanaloo cannot be found. Am I right?"

Alvie nodded. "And…?"

"Aaaand…" But she was at a loss. She sighed heavily. "…I don't see where this is leading. God is everywhere, just like your Oolanaloo. Does that make my God any less important than your Oolanaloo?"

"Oolanaloo is not a god," Alvie said, a calmness in his voice. "No one worships Oolanaloo. No one expects to die and sit beside Oolanaloo in Heaven. No one has to seek out Oolanaloo, because Oolanaloo is everywhere at all times. There is no other than Oolanaloo."

"I think we're arguing semantics," Rene said, on the verge of anger.

Alvie asked, "When bad things happen, do you blame someone or something?"

"Cite me an example," Rene said. *I think I might trip him up on this one*, she thought.

Without any hesitation, Alvie replied, "The deaths of your parents and your husband, and the loss of your son." He looked her square in the eyes.

Anger flashed across her face. "Not fair," she said.

"Why not?"

Now Rene was near tears. "Because you're here to help me with those losses, and I think it's unfair to present those specific examples to me when I'm confused about all of them. Of course I lay blame! Satan himself gave Pop the cancer he suffered. Negligence caused Ma to slip and fall from the wagon and hit her head. The...the weather caused Emmo to die. And as for the death of my unborn son, I blame..." The tears were now cascading down her cheeks like a waterfall.

Alvie reached up and touched her face. There was a tenderness in his touch that Rene hadn't felt since Emmo had left on his last delivery before he died. In addition, something in Alvie's touch awakened a foreign sense within her, one she had never experienced, not even from her parents or Emmo. She hiccupped a couple of breaths, then she felt something in her heart that warmed her. *I think I understand why Alvie presented himself as a child to me. He makes me see things through a child's eyes; I can see them all on a much simpler plane, and there's nothing to stand in the way of the truth. After hearing my own words aloud, I realize how ridiculously absurd it all sounds. And I'm ashamed...honestly ashamed. There is no one to blame and no reason to think so. It all happened simply because it happened.*

Alvie said softly, "I've been through uncountable hard times—wars, pandemics, natural disasters—but the hardest times for me to overcome are individual struggles like yours, Irene." Then he put his arms around Rene's waist and hugged her.

FREEDOM

A couple of weeks passed, and Rene had not seen hide nor hair of Alvie. She guessed that he probably felt she no longer needed him, so he had gone on to tend to others' needs. But she was still unsettled; things were far from being resolved. She harbored doubts about how to overcome some of her undefined feelings, and she was struggling to unravel that.

On the other hand, things were going well with the house. She had heard horror stories about having a house built, but she had not encountered any unpleasant situations. She had been called upon to make certain decisions about some aspects of the building process, but that was to be expected, and not one incident had been unsolvable or unbearable.

The day had been bright and sunny, and there was only a mild breeze that afternoon, not enough to make the waves so big that they would deter her from enjoying the warmth of the sand if she took a barefoot walk on the beach. She sat down on a driftwood log and removed her shoes and stockings. She buried her feet into the sand, threw her head back, closed her eyes, and breathed in as much fresh air as her lungs would hold. She opened her eyes and looked out toward the lake. There, just above the surface of the water, stood Alvie, legs shoulder-distance apart, hands on hips, and a wide grin on his face. Rene smiled and waved, surprised by how elated she was at the sight of him.

He came running across the water toward her, exactly the way a nine-year-old would, if walking on water were a human possibility. When he reached her, he grabbed her by the hands, and the two of them twirled around as if playing a game of ring-around-the-rosey, Alvie laughing the whole time and Rene giggling right along with him. When they stopped, she looked around to see if anyone had seen her, knowing they would think her crazy.

"Don't worry," Alvie said. "I promise, you won't be committed today. No one saw us."

Rene, obviously embarrassed, looked down and said, "I was afraid I'd made a mistake by being so careless. But it made me feel so free."

"'Freedom is not worth having if it does not include the freedom to make mistakes,'[8]" Alvie assured her.

They walked a long way, heading west, picking up things that had washed ashore and examining them as if they might have found some sort of grand treasure. They laughed together, did silly things, and Rene thoroughly enjoyed herself, forgetting all her responsibilities. But the sun was sinking quickly when they decided they'd better turn around and start back. Off to their left, oranges and purples and golds reflected from the ripples of Lake Superior's clear, dark water, and the sun's warmth on Rene's back gave her a feeling of serenity.

"I like you like this," Alvie said.

Rene was somewhat confused by his statement. "Like what?"

"Calm. Untethered by the pull of life's daily routines."

"That's the way I used to feel with Emmo." A smile curled up the corners of her mouth as she remembered their moments of tenderness, alone and unfettered.

Alvie took her hand. "You and Emmo would have walked like this with your son."

And Rene realized, for the first time, that missing them need not always provoke sadness. She stopped and looked down at Alvie. She turned to him, put her hand under his chin, and raised his head so she could look into his eyes. "You have done it, Alvie. You have made me see that there is much satisfaction in my life, even though some of the things I most loved are missing."

The look on Alvie's face was absolute joy in its purest form.

MA AND POP

Rene was sitting in a rocking chair on her porch watching Alvie play Jacks. "Tell me about Ma and Pop."

Alvie knew it would take extra effort to ease Rene's pain attached to the loss of her parents. She had hidden her sadness about their losses so deeply, it was going to require everything he had to help her bring them to the surface and come to grips with feelings she'd repressed for so many years. "Are you sure?" he asked.

"Quite."

"Your pop first, then." Alvie, who had been on his knees, turned toward her and sat cross-legged, being careful to place the little ball in a crack between the boards so it wouldn't roll away. "How much do you know about him?"

"Only that he was a lumberman. And a good provider. He was gone a lot of the time, especially during the winter and spring, and usually a fair portion of the summer. Fall was when he spent the longest time with us. That was always my favorite time. Maybe that's partly why fall is still my favorite season."

Alvie asked, "What kind of man did you perceive him to be? What did he look like? How did his voice sound?" There was an expectant smile on his face.

Rene was aware that Alvie already knew the answers to his questions, and she also knew he was attempting to draw the information out of her, making her say it aloud and getting her used to talking about things with which she was basically uncomfortable, though she had spent years denying that they bothered her. But Alvie's approach had been successful regarding her issues with Emmo and their son, so she was completely at ease with his method for getting her to reveal heretofore unspoken emotions about her parents. She thought for several seconds before answering. "He was purposeful, almost to a fault sometimes, I guess. He…"

Alvie cut her off. "Why 'to a fault'?"

"I can probably count on one hand the times he did something just for fun. Everything had a reason, and that reason was no-nonsense. He wasn't good at playing; maybe he thought play was a waste of time." She looked down at the porch, absentmindedly studying the boards and the precision of the cracks between them. "But he certainly was good at providing for Ma and me." She inhaled loudly through her nose and looked up, as if she had returned to the real world from someplace only she could recognize.

Alvie remained quiet, silently urging her to go on.

"Pop was not a tall man by any stretch of the imagination, but he was muscular. Solid. Built like a brick. His arms and hands were like those of a blacksmith."

She paused in thought before continuing. "He had dark, thick hair and a beard that practically hid his face. His eyes were only slits, and I think they were brown, but I'm not certain; I never paid that much attention to them. He'd always turn his head away when I'd look him square in the face. When I got older, I wondered if it was because he was uncomfortable giving someone—even his own daughter—insight into the emotions he was harboring." She sighed and shook her head. "I never really felt close to him."

Alvie wasn't smiling anymore. He was looking off into the distance.

"As for his voice, it was uncharacteristically soft," she said. "That was the one thing about him I truly loved. He never reprimanded me in a loud tone, nor did he speak to anyone or anything with other than a soft voice. Ma always said he hated bullies and harsh men, and I guess he figured they talked loudly and yelled at people. And that was definitely something he would *not* do."

"So…you figure he was a kind man?" Alvie asked, looking at her.

Rene nodded. "He was. Amiable. Pleasant. Cordial. But not warm; I never saw warmth in him."

She had a far-away look on her face, staring into that place Alvie knew her mind drifted off to when she needed to close off the rest of the world and deeply search things no one else was allowed to share. And he respected that. When she blinked and returned to the moment, Alvie asked, "Do you know anything about his past? Before you were born?"

She shook her head. "Not much. Only that he wasn't from the U.P. Are you willing to fill me in?"

"Didn't your ma ever tell you about him?"

"No. Will you?"

Alvie didn't hesitate. "His life was nothing to be ashamed of," he began. "He was raised in Duluth, up on the side of a hill above the harbor where he could see the ships coming and going all day and all night. When he was only four years old, he fashioned himself to be a sailor. He'd pretend to be the captain of a sailing ship, ordering his crew to raise or lower the sails, to swab the decks, to help guide the ship alongside the docks where they would be filled with all manner of goods to be transported from one end of mighty Lake Superior to the other. Ten years later he boarded one of those ships, and the first mate asked him his age. He pulled himself up to his full height and proudly lied, 'I'm sixteen.' 'So you're looking for work, eh?' the first mate asked. 'Yessir,' your pop said. 'That's too bad,' the first mate answered. 'If you were only fourteen, you could travel as a passenger.' And after making that voyage, being worked harder than he ever thought possible—just like the other sailors aboard—he vowed he'd never lie about his age again." Alvie snorted, and Rene chuckled.

"When the ship arrived along the Pictured Rocks coast east

of Au Sable Point, several of the men disembarked, including your pop. After listening to the talk of the men on board, he abandoned his idea of being a seaman and decided to become a lumberman, just like the men he had come to admire on that voyage. His introduction to the lumbering job came when he was forced to climb up a 300-foot sand dune. It took him nearly half an hour! Can you picture it? For every two feet of progress, he slid back down a foot and a half. But even so, the whole way up, your pop was thinking his future would be magical.

"The men in the Eastern Upper Peninsula logged mostly the white and red pine. Logging up here started in the east and worked its way west, and your pop arrived just as it was becoming prominent right here in Alger County. Those lumbermen realized that all the virgin timber they'd harvest had to get from the top of that dune to the bottom. So they built a wooden chute in order to slide the logs down to the lake for transport. They called it a log *slide* because they could send the logs down and just let gravity do all the work. When those logs took a ride down, they were moving so fast that it only took about ten seconds for them to hit the bottom!"

"I know about that chute. It was really successful; the whole idea of it was pure genius."

"'Success is more a function of consistent common sense than it is of genius,'9" Alvie said.

Rene thought about that. "You're exactly right." Then she asked, "They called it Devil's Slide. Why?"

"It seems it wasn't uncommon for the logs to catch on fire from the friction as they raced toward the bottom. Flames actually rose, along with lots of smoke, both of which could be seen from quite a distance," Alvie explained. "I guess they associated that with what you call Hell."

Rene decided not to pursue that topic any further. "What happened when the logs reached the bottom?" she asked.

"They were collected in what's called a 'boom.' Pine is relatively light and can be floated to mills, so the lumbermen assembled them into rafts for transport across the open lakes."

"Why was Pop gone so much in the winter? How could they

move the trees they cut through all the snow we get here? Obviously, the lake was partially iced over, but the ice couldn't have been strong enough for all that timber. Ships couldn't reach the shoreline, either. I don't understand how it all worked."

"Did you ever see the giant sets of wheels the lumbermen used?" Alvie asked.

Rene nodded. "I never really understood how they worked, though."

"Those wheels, most of which are ten feet in diameter, were used to pull logs from the forests where they'd been harvested. Because of their size, the wheels had a very high axle, so they could get through just about any land surface without getting bogged down."

"They could go over stumps, through swamps, and through snow," Rene said, proud of herself for recognizing the connection.

Alvie continued. "That's right. A team of either oxen or horses pulled them. Before the wheels were invented, the logs had to be 'skidded' out to the main logging roads, and that was really tough work, especially when they had to go through a section of clear-cut forest and maneuver around and over all of the stumps. After the invention of the big wheels, the logs could be moved much easier, whether there was snow or not. When the timber reached the roads, it was loaded onto wagons in the warmer months and sleighs in winter and hauled to the riverbanks or, like the Pictured Rocks lakeshore, to the tops of the dunes where it was stored until spring. The really interesting part is that, here in the U.P., the winter was used to their advantage because they could transport the timber to the tops of the dunes on ice roads, which were actually a Michigan innovation. Men ran a sprinkler over a logging road during the cold nights, and by morning, all of the ruts and rough places in the road had become sheets of ice so the horses or oxen could pull the log-laden sleighs over them easier.

"Then, in the spring when the lake ice melted, the logs were sent down the chute and assembled into rafts that went to Munising Bay, Au Train Bay, Grand Marais, Sault Sainte Marie, and eventually even further on down the lakes. Then they were arranged into booms and towed away. Some of them went to Garden Island, Ontario, where they were squared and shipped to Liverpool, England. Sometimes there was as much as 150,000 square feet of lumber shipped out! But I'm getting ahead of myself. Sorry." It was obvious that Alvie could tell Rene was completely wrapped up in his story about her father's work; nevertheless, he politely asked if he should continue. "Am I boring you?"

"Please don't stop," Rene begged.

"Well, you can imagine that the rafting process could be a major problem on the waters of the Great Lakes, considering the storms that pop up so unexpectedly."

"They're treacherous at times," Rene said, her eyes big as saucers, thinking about her father being caught in the middle of Superior during one of them.

"Your father never accompanied the rafts," he assured her.

She let out a sigh of relief. "Thank goodness! Go on."

"The rafts sometimes had to travel as much as 200 miles, and it was obvious that a new boom system had to be developed. The solution was to drill holes in super big pine logs, most of them three or four feet in diameter, and thread them together with heavy logging chain, which created a sort of fence that floated. And the 'fence' surrounded a whole bunch of smaller logs that stayed put within the much larger ones that were hooked together. Now this blows my mind..."

"It what?" Rene asked.

He paused to think about what he'd said. "Nevermind. Sometimes the floating logs covered as much as twenty acres. And from the air, they looked like big balloons being pulled behind the ships. It was *awesome!*" He closed his eyes and blushed. "I know you'll never see them, but trust me, they were unbelievable. The amount of logs that were moved in such a short timespan is nearly inconceivable. Just one year before you were born, thirty million feet of logs were rafted from Lake Superior down through Lake Huron—thirty million; do you realize how many that is? One time an eight-million-square-foot raft was taken to

Alpena."

Rene knew Alvie was excited, and that made her all the more interested in what her father had been a part of. "Exactly what did Pop do?" she asked.

Alvie's voice changed; he sounded highly respectful when he said, "He was one of the most important members of the logging crew. He was a teamster."

Rene frowned.

"He drove the horses. The camp boss realized how soft-spoken your pop was, so he knew the horses would respond well to your pop. And that was lucky for him, because it meant he got to stay in separate quarters, *much* nicer than the rest of the men. It also meant he earned twice as much pay per day, which was two dollars instead of the one dollar most of them earned."

"That explains why he was such a good provider," Rene said. "And I never would have guessed that his nature dictated his position."

Alvie allowed her a few moments to digest all he had just told her, then he said, "His eyes were brown. Just like yours."

Rene looked at him and smiled, her gratitude apparent. "Thank you," she said. "And now Ma. I was much closer to her, but that doesn't mean I know much more about her. I know she was Finnish, but I don't think she ever lived in Finland. Her parents came to the United States before she was born. Is that right?"

"Yes," Alvie said.

"She had more courage, more stoicism and determination than I ever saw in another woman. She was resilient. Hardy, I guess you'd say."

"Sisu." Alvie said.

Rene's mouth dropped open. "She had that word written on a piece of paper tucked into the corner of the mirror on her dressing table. I've never known what it meant."

"You just defined it."

"I...I don't understand," Rene said.

"Did you ever see her fail to accomplish what she set out to do? Was she ever lacking in tenacity?"

Rene thought about it, and a smile slowly appeared on her

face. "Sisu."

"That was your ma. I'll tell you a story about her that even makes *me* smile," Alvie said. "Every year in the spring and late fall your pop would take your ma to the lumber camp for a few days."

"Yes, I remember that; I used to have to stay at Pearl's house when they went. I think Ma was going to do some sewing, maybe some washing. Is that right?"

"Exacta Mundo."

Rene looked at him with a blank stare.

Alvie blushed again and cleared his throat. "Yes. You are right."

She rolled her eyes and shook her head.

"The men wore long underwear all winter, of course. Each had their initials sewn into the skivvies when they were new. They never took them off to bathe until the weather was warm enough to shed the underwear, at which time the ones not completely worn out were thrown into one pile to be washed, and the unusable ones went into another pile to be burned. At each lumber camp, there was a huge cast iron pot used exclusively for doing laundry twice a year—once in the spring, and once in the late fall. Each of the men was required to carry two buckets of water from the nearest source and dump their contents into the pot. A fire was then built around the ginormous…uh, giant….pot to heat the water for washing and to burn the discarded items of clothing.

"Your ma's responsibility was to launder the reusable underwear and sew each man's initials into the new items the men had bought from the camp store. She also replaced any missing buttons on the used skivvies, both front and back, if necessary. But she only did that *after* they had been washed. I'm sure you understand why."

Rene wrinkled her nose, squinted her eyes, and said, "Bleuach!"

"My sentiments, as well," Alvie said. "Well, one year a new man at the camp came up to your ma and shoved a pair of unwashed underwear at her, saying, 'I need a button sewed on da backdoor o' dese.' Your ma, without missing a beat said, 'Not on your life.'"

Rene was smiling broadly.

"'Whadda ya mean?' the man asked. 'I tawt you was here ta do da sewin'.' Your ma stared right into the man's eyeballs and, mocking his accent, said, 'An' I tawt a lumberman had ta be smarter dan 'is axe!'" Alvie threw his head back and laughed with complete abandon.

Rene wasn't certain she comprehended the total significance of the story, but seeing Alvie so consumed by laughter caused her broad smile to turn into a grin. And within a couple of seconds, the contagion overtook her, and she began to laugh too. Before long, she and Alvie were exhibiting unabashed hilarity, the likes of which she had only ever experienced with Emmo on rare occasions.

When the laughter finally abated, Alvie said softly, "'As soap is to the body, so laughter is to the soul.'[10]"

1936

PEARL'S DILEMMA

Rene spent the early portion of her day sitting at her picture window facing Lake Superior. She watched the gulls soaring over the low breakers, the fishing boats coming and going, and the fishermen casting their nets. Whenever it was sunny and the water was relatively calm, like that day, she could just make out the shapes of the ore carriers passing by, far out on the horizon.

Grand Marais had been experiencing a new kind of prosperity called tourism. In the 1920s a state road, M-77, had opened an easy way to get from US-2 in the southern part of the U.P. to Grand Marais in the north. This offered beautiful scenery to outsiders, and more and more of them seemed happy to take advantage of the opportunity now that the run on the banks (the Great Depression) was easing up.

Alvie continued to live in Rene's attic when he was not guiding another subject somewhere else in the universe or in some other timeframe. He was often gone for weeks on end, but he always returned, and that pleased Rene. *Maybe because it gives me something to look forward to*, she thought. She moved from the window to the warmth of the steps leading up to the small stoop at the front of the house. Alvie, who had returned the night before, came around the corner by the big maple tree and sat down on the step beside her. She greeted him with a smile but said nothing because she saw Pearl coming down the street toward her. She waved at Pearl. Alvie followed Pearl with his eyes.

"What brings you by this gorgeous morning?" she asked Pearl.

"Garnet," Pearl said, agitation obvious in her voice. She was not smiling.

Rene closed her eyes, sighed, and shook her head. "What's she up to now?"

Pearl looked off into the distance, as if she might find an answer there. "She wants me to sell the boarding house and move in with her so I can take care of her. Says she's too old to take care of herself anymore and that it's my duty to care for her since I have no one else to be responsible for."

Rene's jaw dropped open.

"She's old and feeble; I know that," Pearl said. "But I can't imagine being responsible for her until, well, until she dies. She's so cantankerous." She rolled her eyes. "She'll probably outlive me, most likely because taking care of her will kill me."

Rene stifled a snicker. "But you just finished paying for the boarding house. It's yours now, free and clear."

Pearl's shoulders slumped, and she looked at Rene with the saddest expression Rene had ever seen on her friend's face. "Rene, the days of making any profit by running a boarding house are numbered. People aren't interested in staying there. The trend is moving more toward auto camps, cabin courts, tourist homes, even travel trailers. People don't want to stay someplace long term; they want to keep moving. I recently read in a travel magazine that there's a place in California called a mo-tel—a motor hotel—where people can stay for just one night and then move on. Every room faces a parking lot, so every room has its own door directly to the outside. And there's a bathroom in every room, too. If tourism continues to grow, it looks like motels might become the perfect thing for travelers. I couldn't possibly borrow enough to convert the boarding house to one of those. And I don't have enough land to provide adequate parking anyway."

Rene knew Pearl was ready to cry. "Oh, Pearl. I had no idea you'd been stewing over this. How long ago did Garnet present you with her request?"

"A little over a month," she said, her voice nearly inaudible. "I've been reading everything I can about the changes in tourism, and I don't see any profitable way to make my situation work."

"Then sell it," Rene said.

Pearl threw her hands into the air. "Who's going to buy a dead-end business that has no hope of becoming successful? I can't afford to update to modern amenities. I spent so much on the two indoor bathrooms three years ago, I'd have to ask an exorbitant price for the place, just to break even. The run on the banks really put a strain on me because people stopped traveling…well, other than the incredibly wealthy. And the traveling salesmen." Tears were now streaming down her face, leaving glistening trails on her cheeks. "I'm pretty much destitute, Rene, and Garnet knows that. That's why she wants me to move in with her. She says she has enough money for the two of us to get by—apparently funds are not an issue by her estimation. But she wants me to let the boarding house go."

"You know I'd be willing to help you financially," Rene said.

"And you know my stand on borrowing from a friend," Pearl said. "The fastest way to destroy a friendship is to make your friend a business partner."

"Yes, I know," Rene said. She rose, walked up to Pearl, and hugged her.

Pearl squeaked through her sobs, "But thank you for your offer anyway."

Rene took her dearest friend by the hand and said, "I'll put on a pot of coffee, and we can try to work out the details of your dilemma. We'll sit in the back yard. It's a beautiful day, and that view, along with the sunshine, always makes me think more clearly. You go on around to the back, and I'll be out in a few minutes."

She went to the kitchen to start the coffee and saw that Pearl had seated herself on one of the wooden Adirondack chairs. She could feel someone in the room, so she turned, and there was Alvie standing directly behind her. "What can I do to help her?" she asked him. "I'm only asking for your opinion. I don't expect you to break any rules or do anything drastic."

Alvie thought for a moment, then he said, "'Every man is working out his destiny in his own way, and nobody can be of any help except by being kind, generous, and patient.'[11] I know that's the sort of person *you* are, Irene, and I think you should take that to heart."

Eventually Rene went outside with the coffee. On the small table between the two Adirondack chairs she placed a tray holding a cream pitcher, a sugar bowl, two spoons, two napkins, and two cups of coffee sitting on saucers, one of which she handed to Pearl. Then she sat down in the other chair. "If it were me, I think I'd need to sleep a little longer on all of this before making any decisions. I'm aware that you've been thinking about it for the past month, but another few days and nights might make a difference since there's so much to consider. And together, we might come up with some new ideas to add to the list."

"That's probably smart," Pearl said, nodding. "But Garnet is not doing well, so I feel obligated to take care of her in the meantime."

"And that's quite understandable. I think you need not move into her house, though, until you've taken care of your own affairs first."

Pearl's attitude lightened. "You're right. I do have my own life to straighten out, and I'm glad you agree with what I've been thinking all along. It's not that I don't want to care for Garnet. She *is* my sister, after all. But the thought of moving in with her has been a pebble in my shoe. Thank you for allowing me to see that you think the same way I've been thinking. You truly are a good friend." She reached over and touched Rene's arm.

Alvie was seated on the ground in front of Pearl, watching her and obviously soaking up the emotional relief he could see her experiencing. Back in the kitchen while the coffee was perking, he had told Rene he thought Pearl was being pulled too many directions at once and needed more time before deciding whether to move in with Garnet. He offered some suggestions and urged Rene to present them to Pearl.

Rene said, "I know it always helps me to follow something I've written down; that way I don't get wrapped up in one thing and forget about some other important thing I need to accomplish. What would you think of making a schedule for yourself so you can evenly divide your time between your own affairs and the time necessary to dedicate to Garnet?"

Alvie had also told Rene that Opal felt a bit left out because Garnet had not requested her assistance. So Rene presented the option of asking for Opal's help, and Pearl agreed to talk to Opal about it. "Maybe the two of you together could work out a doable schedule," Rene said. Opal's husband had been a dredger, and he had died two years ago in a terrible accident while on the job. The dredging company was supporting Opal financially, so she had some income, but she was planning to move to St. Ignace where she had been offered a job by a bank there. It was a good job, and she told Pearl she couldn't afford not to take it; however, it wouldn't become available until the current employee retired, and that wouldn't be for another four months.

When they finished their coffee, Pearl rose to leave and said, "I can't thank you enough for helping me with all of this. I don't know why I was struggling with it so."

"You're simply too close to it all. You know the old expression, 'You can't see the forest for the trees?' That's exactly what it's been with you, I think."

"I'm looking forward to talking to Opal about it. I think she'll be more than happy to comply until it's time for her move."

Rene followed Pearl around to the front of the house. They looked out on the town, both silently taking in the changes they had seen in the place they'd called home throughout the years. Rene was pleased with what she saw. She felt the changes had been for the better.

Once again, Pearl put her arm around her friend. She looked at the ground and said, "I need to concentrate on making Garnet's life as happy as possible. Just a couple of Sundays ago, our minister said, 'The best way to find yourself is to lose yourself in the service of others.'[12]"

Rene smiled; she could see Alvie smiling as well.

REFLECTING

Rene loved hearing Alvie talk about the history of her town. He told her, "Grand Marais has one of the oldest place-names on the Great Lakes. It's French, and it means *great marsh*."

Rene frowned. "But there's never been a marsh around Grand Marais."

"Yeah, I know. Historians have decided that mapmakers probably confused it with a similar-sounding French word, *m-a-r-é*," which he spelled and pronounced aloud, and Rene was impressed by his French accent. "It means *sheltered body of water*," Alvie said.

"I had no idea. I simply never even thought about it," Rene said, almost embarrassed by her confession. "Please tell me more."

"The Native Americans were the first modern settlers here. They were mostly Chippewas, and they were here because of the abundance of beavers. Do you know the name John Jacob Astor?"

"I certainly do! Pop spoke of him. Didn't he establish some kind of fur trading company?

"The American Fur Company."

"That's the name of the outpost that was here in Grand Marais, right?" Rene asked.

Alvie nodded. "Its headquarters were on Mackinac Island, but there were lots of other fur companies that came and went around the Great Lakes." He changed his train of thought. "What year is this again?"

"1936."

"Aha! Are you aware of the Pickle Barrel House?"[13]

Rene said excitedly, "Yes! I heard it's being moved into town."

"Uh-huh," Alvie said. "It sure is a strange building."

"I think it'll become an attraction here in Grand Marais. I can imagine people coming here just to see it. Of course, they'll be overwhelmed by our beautiful place on the lake, but it certainly can't hurt to have a gimmick to lure them in, can it?"

"Why, Mrs. Vandersligh, you have quite the enterprising mind," Alvie teased. Again, he shifted his attention to another subject. "Do you remember Grand Marais being a U.S. Life-Saving Station before it became part of the Coast Guard?"

"Barely. I was pretty much involved in other things at that point," she said, blushing.

"Oh yeah. Emmo," Alvie said, and Rene nodded, a faraway look on her face and a smile on her lips. Alvie could see the memories running through her head. He gave her time to reminisce before continuing. "It existed along with Deer Park, Two Heart, Crisp Point, and Vermillion Point. There had been a huge increase in boat traffic, and the shipwrecks increased at the same rate, so a lifesaving station was built at the foot of Grand Marais's west pier in 1898."

Rene smiled; she knew Alvie was excited to talk about such things.

"And when it was completed, it was considered one of the finest on all of the Great Lakes. The station had a 34-foot lifeboat that was self-righting, two surf boats, and all the beach gizmos you can imagine."

"What's a beach gizmo?"

Alvie looked at her with a blank expression. "Nevermind."

"Weren't they the men who went out in horrible weather and rescued people from shipwrecks?"

"Yep. They risked their own lives to save others. Those were some courageous men. They were fearless!" he said. "'Fearlessness is like a muscle…the more you exercise it, the more natural it becomes to not let your fears run you.'[14]"

"You didn't just make that up, did you?" Rene asked.

"No," Alvie admitted. "A woman you don't know, from the future, is responsible for it."

She sighed. "I sometimes wish I could jump back and forth the way you do. Do you suppose…"

"Strictly against the rules," Alvie said quite matter-of-factly.

"Why have you chosen to stay here, Alvie? With me, I mean. I'm guessing you've helped others who are far more interesting. Why not stay with them?" she asked.

Alvie gave her that tender smile of his, accompanied by a slight tilt of his head. "Because I like this point in time. I like this particular place here on earth. I like your house—your attic." He blushed. "And…" he paused, looking deeply into her eyes,

"...I like you."

PROBLEM SOLVED

Nearly a week had passed since Pearl had presented her dilemma to Rene. Rene was busy tidying up the kitchen when she heard a knock at her back door. She opened it to see Pearl's smiling face. "Well, don't you look like the cat who swallowed the canary," Rene said, inviting her best friend in.

They sat down, and Pearl, who was obviously excited, said, "I'm so glad I took your suggestion. I made a daily schedule, *and* I talked to Opal. When I talked to you last, I was feeling really sorry for myself, I must admit. Opal and I were sitting in my office in the boarding house in the midst of trying to figure out how we could share the duties of taking care of Garnet when there was a knock at my office door." She stopped, obviously waiting for Rene to ask her to go on. Rene obliged.

"Well, a man came in, sat down, and said he was a developer and was interested in the boarding house property. He told me he'd like to buy it and turn it into a 'cabin court.' He said he understood that Grand Marais was becoming…um… Oh, what did he call it?" She put her hand on her head and frowned. "A tourist mecca!" she exploded.

That's wonderful!" Rene said.

Pearl reached out and put her hand on Rene's arm. "There's more, and this is where it gets really good." Pearl was so excited; Rene could almost feel electrical impulses coming through her hand. "Opal thinks it would be a good idea for her to sell her house, and for the two of us to live in Garnet's house—it has three bedrooms—while the project is taking place. Since Opal's Edgar died, she's been lonely living in her house all by herself. And…" She paused long enough to catch her breath. "…the man also said he'd like to rent my house while the work is going on so he has a place he can call his headquarters. His rent would give me some steady income. Then, when his job is completed, I can move back into my house and sell Garnet's big place and divide those profits up with Opal and Ruby."

Rene allowed Pearl to go on and on, all the while knowing

that, approximately a week ago, Alvie had been aware of what was about to take place when he had urged Rene to suggest to Pearl that waiting a little longer before making any decisions was the best way to handle the situation. Pearl was talking faster and faster, "He says he's planning to tear down the old boarding house completely and build four or five cabins. He wants to make two of them big enough to hold a whole family. They would have two beds or maybe even one double bed and bunk beds for the kids. Isn't that just a wonderful idea?"

"It certainly is," Rene said, mirroring Pearl's excitement. Pearl talked more about the plans the developer had shared with her, and finally Rene asked, "I guess the real question is, did he offer you a fair price?"

Pearl beamed. "That's the best part. Not only is he giving me more than I was going to ask for it, he says his development company will give it all to me in one lump sum! Do you believe it?"

"Have you talked to a lawyer?"

"Yes. As soon as the man left, I made an appointment with a lawyer in Sault Ste. Marie who specializes in land development. He said he's been involved in other work this same development company has done. The things the developer said to me are all above board, and the lawyer said I should accept the offer." She was just shy of being giddy.

"Oh, Pearl. I can't tell you how happy it makes me to see you this thrilled." Then Rene quietly asked, "Have you mentioned it to Garnet?"

"Not a word. She's so self-absorbed she wouldn't be the least bit interested anyway. In fact—and I probably shouldn't say this—I don't think her mind is even capable of grasping the whole thing." Pearl lowered her eyes, avoiding Rene's. "I don't know how long it's been since you've communicated with her."

"Probably over a year," Rene admitted.

"Oh, my. Then you aren't aware of her condition. She's been going steadily downhill since last November."

"You mean she's deteriorating mentally?"

Pearl nodded and raised her head, meeting Rene's concerned

expression.

With her voice soft and low, Rene asked, "Does she still know everyone?"

"She knows us: Opal, Ruby, and me, I mean. I'm not sure how well she does with other people, though from the sounds of it, I don't think she has many visitors. She doesn't go to church, so I'm certain none of our friends seek her company. I honestly can't name one person I know who has been to her house over the past several months." Pearl closed her eyes. "I'm ashamed of that, and it makes me sad to think of her loneliness."

They chatted a bit longer before Pearl said, "I need to go. It's about time for me to meet with the developer and sign the papers."

COMING TO GRIPS

Deep in her heart of hearts Rene knew she should take pity on Garnet, but it was simply too difficult to overcome her perception of the woman's behavior throughout the years. And, of course, there were the lingering feelings she harbored about Garnet's actions with Emmo so long ago. *Why can't I get that out of my mind?* she thought. *It has absolutely no bearing on my current wellbeing. I know I'm supposed to forgive and forget, but as desperately as I try, I cannot, because Garnet brought it on herself.*

"Are humans really capable of doing that?" Alvie asked.

Rene jumped. He had read her thoughts. She didn't begrudge him doing so, though sometimes she felt a portion of her privacy was being invaded, and this was one of those times.

"Sorry," Alvie said apologetically.

"I just can't stop thinking that Garnet has been a taker all of her life. Am I wrong?"

"No. And yes."

Rene sighed. She knew a lesson was coming.

"You don't have to listen to another lesson," Alvie said with the faintest hint of an embarrassed smile.

"I just…it's just that…"

"Bad timing on my part," he said, extending his arms and holding his hands out in front of him. "I should have given you more time to come to grips with your feelings. That's one of the things I like best about you: you have an undeniable ability to reason—something a great number of humans lack. Please accept my apology."

"I don't know how you manage to make me feel good and bad all at the same time, and yet, the good always seems to float to the surface."

"It's my job. It's what I do. It's how I make a living." He grinned. "Although that last part is pretty much a moot point for me."

Rene smiled and shook her head.

Alvie said, "You did a great job making Pearl feel good about herself again."

"Only because you gave me the opportunity to set myself up for it."

Alvie's brow furrowed.

Rene said, "You're the one who suggested I advise her about making a schedule, talking to Opal, keeping herself focused."

Alvie said, "But *you* are the one who delivered the message. And Pearl didn't shoot the messenger." He raised his head and sniffed the air like a dog. "Do I smell popcorn?"

1942

WHAT'S IN A NAME?

Rene kept her radio on throughout the day, only turning it off to sleep at night. She couldn't believe what she had been hearing about Hitler's Nazi regime and their abhorrent treatment of non-Nazi people, especially Jews. And there didn't seem to be anything anyone could do to stop it. Rene had only recently become aware of Alvie's name sounding Jewish. "Didn't you tell me once that you chose your own name?" she asked him.

Alvie, who had been moping around for days, nodded but didn't speak.

Rene was stumped. "But I thought you had no cultural preference."

Alvie stared blankly at nothing in particular and didn't respond, so Rene didn't press the issue. She continued dusting the items on the upper shelves of the big hutch Emmo had bought for her shortly after they'd gotten married; it was the only piece of furniture she'd kept when she moved back to Grand Marais.

After several minutes, Alvie asked, "Why do you do it?"

She jumped at the sound of his voice. "Well, dust collects on the pieces of…"

"No, not the dusting," Alvie said. "The killing."

Rene froze. "I don't understand, Alvie. I've never killed anyone." Thoughts began to race through her mind. *Why would he ask me that? Does he think I killed my child? Or Emmo? What does he mean?* "I don't understand," she repeated.

"Not you, personally, Irene. Humans, in general."

She sighed, partly in relief and partly because she knew he expected an answer, and she wasn't sure she was going to be able to provide one. She put the dusting rag down and pulled a chair away from the dining table; she sat down and placed her hands in her lap. Then she looked at the young person sitting across from her. He appeared so vulnerable, his facial expression drooping, his shoulders sagging. "I'm afraid that's a question no individual can truthfully answer."

Tears welled in Alvie's eyes, and his lower lip quivered.

Rene had not witnessed such despair from the boy before her. "This is related to what you've been hearing on the radio, isn't it?" But she reminded herself that Alvie had been through it all before. He had known what was happening, what had already happened, and what was yet to come. Rene was woefully aware, however, that his knowing didn't make it easier for him to face it each time he encountered it.

He said, "I chose my name so I'd never forget what happened—happens—during this period on your planet. I wanted to do one little thing that might honor all those poor people who were..." he stopped and looked into Rene's eyes.

She felt a chill run though her. In a soft, soothing voice, she asked him, "Why have you chosen to go through this again, Alvie? You have the option to skip this entire era, yet here you are with me, sitting at my dining table, putting yourself through what appears to be total agony when you could..."

He cut her off. "I am here to guide you. I cannot do that if I skip over this monumental event in your history." He shifted uncomfortably in his seat. "Unfortunately, I've been forced to live through it thousands of times in order to guide others through it. It saddens me more than anything else I've ever encountered anywhere in my travels. And I have encountered it over and over and over..." his voice trailed off, his eyes clouded with more grief, and he disappeared.

Rene didn't know what to think. *Have I let him down? Does he need <u>me</u> now more than I've needed him? If so, then I've failed <u>him</u>. What did I do to make him so melancholy, so hopeless, when I only wanted to ease his sorrow?* She was beside herself with distress over the matter. She rose, walked to the radio, and angrily turned it off.

HELL ON EARTH

The United States was struggling over its own relationships with the rest of the world. Names that were foreign to Rene and places she had never heard of kept invading her thoughts. She was slowly being beaten down by the talk of Allied Powers, Axis Powers, Imperial Japan, Fascist Italy. But the worst of all was stories about the concentration camps. She heard and read about places called Bergen-Belsen in Germany, Auschwitz-Birkenau in Poland, Terezin in Czechoslovakia.

Four months passed, and Alvie had not reappeared. Rene needed him now more than ever. She was consumed with the news about the United States and Europe and Japan and Russia and North Africa. She could not sleep, could not get the bad visions out of her head, could not get through a day without crying. But she knew Alvie had been guiding others who needed him even more. She couldn't help but think that perhaps she had done or said something that had made him feel unwelcome in her home—well, her attic—and her life.

She looked up; Alvie was standing in front of her. He greeted her without smiling. "Hello, Irene."

"Oh, Alvie, I've missed you so." She took a step toward him but stopped short. "I know you were needed elsewhere, but I couldn't help thinking…"

"I'm back only for a short visit. And I have news: I spoke with Oolanaloo. You may accompany me on my next trip to Europe, if you still want to."

Rene was speechless. She could only stare at Alvie, her lower jaw hanging slack, her mind totally befuddled.

"It won't be easy," Alvie said, a strange seriousness in his voice. "I mean, it won't be easy to grasp what you will see. And what you see will stay with you for the remainder of your days."

Rene swallowed and said, "I thought you said I couldn't…"

"You can't travel through time or other dimensions, but Oolanaloo says you may travel with me to another place in your own time. You may witness the things that are torturing you. Seeing them will keep you from wondering about them and conjuring up your own ideas about what the people are enduring."

"Why would you do that for me?" she asked.

"I am here to guide you, and I know that you can only find peace if you truly understand, firsthand, what's happening on the other side of the world, not just believing what you read or hear in your own little corner of it. Oolanaloo agrees."

Rene straightened up to her full height and said, "If you feel this is something I should do, I will do it. I trust you, Alvie. I trust that you know what's best for me."

"It's Oolanaloo you must trust." His eyes were dark and conveyed genuine gravity that Rene had not seen in them before. She nodded. Alvie took her by the hand, and they were instantly standing in a strange place. It was night, and there was a cloying odor hanging in the air—one she didn't recognize—pungent and unpleasant. She waited for her eyes to adjust, but she could see nothing familiar except a small sliver of the moon, the same moon that hung over Lake Superior. But she was not near her lake. She tightened her grip on Alvie's hand.

A bright white light shone in her eyes, and the distant sounds of an approaching train became apparent. *This must be a train station,* she thought. *I haven't heard that sound for a long time.* Its familiarity made her feel comfortable, reminding her of the days when Grand Marais was the end of the line for the logging trains.

She blinked, and she and Alvie were standing atop a low building, looking down on the train as it rolled to a stop before them, the engine smoking and hissing and the wheels screeching metallically along the tracks. It was late November, and the air was cold and biting. Rene could see a thin film of snow covering the ground below them, reflecting the pale bit of moonlight enough to brighten up the surroundings ever so slightly.

Military-uniformed men carrying rifles emerged from the building on which she and Alvie were standing. The soldiers separated, several going to each of the boxcars that trailed behind the locomotive. The soldiers barked orders in a language Rene didn't recognize, and doors on each side of the cars slid open. Rene was expecting to see crates and boxes inside each car, but she saw only people, packed into the cars like sardines. They were of all ages. Some were dressed in fine clothes, some in rags, some being supported by others, some carrying small children, some wearing winter coats and hats, others without. All of them began climbing down out of the train cars and descending the ramps that were positioned beside each car.

"Look at the patches they wear," Alvie said. "Can you see them on the front of their clothes?"

She looked closely and could just make out a six-pointed star on the chests of the people who were exposed in the moonlight, the ones standing outside the shadows of the train cars. Whispering, she asked, "What does it say on the stars?"

"Different things. But they identify the people as Jews. The star is the Hebrew Star of David. The people are required to wear it where it can be conspicuously seen. Different colors signify different things, too." He didn't elaborate, and Rene didn't question him further.

After two or three minutes of watching the soldiers forcefully separating the men and women and children, she concluded that Alvie had brought her to one of the Nazi concentration camps. And she closed her eyes when the realization that the odor she had smelled upon their arrival was the lingering scent from "the showers"—the furnaces. "Take me back home," she ordered Alvie. "Now!"

They were instantly standing in Rene's kitchen. Tears slipped from her eyes. She didn't blink. She didn't move. She just stood there, silently crying, shivering, and unable to accurately interpret what she had witnessed only seconds ago. And she knew those people's tribulations had only begun. *How do they deal with it?* She wondered. *How do they cope with the mystery of what's happening to them?*

"They don't," Alvie said, his voice barely audible.

Rene looked at him, knowing he had read her thoughts.

"Some of them—most of them, actually—don't even know what their fate will be. And for that, we can be relieved. But the relief is short-lived, because they find out all too soon."

"Which camp was that?"

"Birkenau," Alvie said. "I'll be taking you again."

Rene closed her eyes, and panic caused a surge of adrenaline to course through her. "Now?" her voice quivered.

"No, but soon."

"Why do I need to go back?"

"To understand." And with that, he disappeared, leaving Rene wondering what she was destined to understand.

She decided to find out as much as she possibly could about the Nazis. She began by reluctantly turning her radio back on, knowing that the only station she could pick up would be broadcasting every bit of news the foreign reporters could find to send back to the United States. She purchased every newspaper she could find, though many of the articles were the same in several of the papers because of syndication. She talked to all her friends around town, bringing up the subject as subtly as possible, gently easing it into conversations, but the facts she gleaned were few and far between. She knew it was difficult for anyone to expound upon the subject, not only because it was so sensitive, but also because there were few facts available, though there was plenty of conjecture.

After a few days, Alvie returned. His mood had not improved; if anything, he was more dejected than he'd been when he left her after their previous trip to Europe. "Oolanaloo says we must visit again." With that, he took her hand, and the two of them were at Auschwitz, standing within the fences that surrounded one of the blocks, the areas of buildings used for housing. No one could see the two of them standing there. "You must not let go my hand, or you will become visible. You don't have the ability to remain unseen without our constant contact."

Rene nodded, unable to look at Alvie because she could not avert her eyes from the ambulatory skeletons around her, none with adequate clothing, all moving to try and keep themselves from freezing. They were all men, and except for variations in height, they all looked alike. In the absence of muscle mass, their faces and bodies consisted only of skin covering their frames. Hairless heads contained dark eye sockets with no emotion evident in the eyes deep within them. Every rib was exposed over a concave belly. Knees and elbows protruded. Bare feet, appearing overly long and flat, clung from the ends of leg bones by only a thread of skin. Bony hands with elongated fingers reminded Rene of drawings she had seen depicting the Devil's henchmen who came to snatch sinful souls and force them into the depths of Hell.

"That's exactly where we are," Alvie said.

"You believe in Hell?" Rene asked him.

"No, but you Christian humans do, and this is what you imagine it to be, right?"

She looked around again and decided there was no arguing the fact, so she remained silent.

"We must all learn to live together as brothers, or we will all perish together as fools,"[15] Alvie said, discernible gloom in his voice. She momentarily closed her eyes, no longer able to tolerate the sight before her. When she opened them, she was standing in her living room. The person holding her hand was not a nine-year-old boy; instead, it was a tall, slender man, about 50 years of age, with thick salt-and-pepper hair, and he was dressed in a nice pair of dark pants and a starched white shirt, open at the neck. She released the man's hand and asked, "Who are you?"

"It's me, Irene. Alvie."

"No. Alvie is only nine. He's a boy."

Alvie tilted his head and smiled tenderly at her, like he always did when she needed to be comforted. Rene squinted and looked deeply into the man's eyes. The familiarity was evident. "It *is* you! But…why…why have you changed?" She was on the verge of tears.

"Think about what you just saw. Would you truly consider discussing that with a child?"

Her brow furrowed, and a painful expression overtook her face. She walked to her davenport and plopped down, her legs no longer able hold her up. She was breathing heavily, her face tortuously distorted. "But…I don't…"

"You have become accustomed to seeing me as a child. Now that you have witnessed such horror, however, you need an adult to talk to. You may not even realize it, but up till now you have assumed the role of parent with me. It's time for us to renew our friendship...as adult friends."

Rene's facial expression softened. She swallowed hard and looked at the new Alvie standing there beside her. *His appearance is pleasant enough, non-threatening.*

"Don't think of me as someone else. Think of me simply as grown-up Alvie. I'm still the same person, Irene. I haven't changed inside. I just know, from experience, that you'll be able to open up to me more easily if you see me as an adult. You'll more readily talk to me about adult things and adult feelings."

She knew he was right, though she couldn't help admitting, "But I'll miss Alvie the boy."

Alvie put his hand on his chest. "Alvie the boy is still right here."

LILIANA BARTOSZ

Early on a cold and snowy morning, Rene heard a light knock at her door. She opened it and was pleasantly surprised to see Pearl standing there. "Come in here before you freeze to death," Rene said, moving aside so Pearl could pass by on her way in.

But Pearl didn't move. She looked straight ahead, not up at Rene's face, and said, "She's dead."

It took a couple of seconds before Rene realized Pearl was talking about Garnet. "Oh, Pearl. I'm so sorry to hear..."

"Don't be," Pearl said. "God was only prolonging her misery. And mine." She pushed past Rene and took off her gloves, then her hat, absentmindedly handing them to Rene. Then she began unbuttoning her long coat. The warmth of Rene's house was quickly melting the snow that had accumulated on the coat's dark green wool. Rene waited patiently while Pearl methodically slipped each button through its corresponding buttonhole and eventually was able to pull her arms out of the garment and hand it, unconsciously, to Rene.

"Was it a peaceful death?" Rene asked her friend.

"Yes. It was during the night, in her sleep. I can't decide if she deserved to go so easily."

"That's God's choice, not ours," Rene said.

Pearl hung her head, and her shoulders heaved up and down as she sobbed. "I'm sorry. I'm just so tired. And angry. And relieved."

Rene embraced the woman she'd been closest to for half a century. She was glad Pearl felt comfortable enough to voice her true opinions without having to justify her feelings. "You have spent too many hours and too much energy for too long. You have gone above and beyond the call of duty caring for that woman, Pearl."

Pearl put her arms around Rene's waist and buried her head in the front of her best friend's dress. Tears ran from Pearl's eyes like water from an upended bucket, and Rene knew it wasn't sorrow at their source; it was pure release secondary to the emancipation of the responsibility of caring for such a difficult person for such an extended period of time. Rene was momentarily ashamed at feeling no sincere grief for Garnet, only for Pearl.

When Pearl was finally able to regain her composure, she pulled a handkerchief from her skirt pocket and wiped her face. "I didn't know I had so many tears left to cry," she said, apparently embarrassed.

"A good cry is exactly what you needed in order to let go of things you've held inside all this time," Rene comforted her.

"You're right." Pearl blew out a huff of air. "I already feel several hundred percent better." She even smiled.

"I was just about to scramble some eggs, and I have a pot of coffee going. You'll join me, won't you?"

"Have you ever known me to turn down your cooking?"

"Hmmm…" Rene put her hand on her chin. "Now that you mention it, I can't recall that ever happening."

Pearl straightened up. "I know there's a lot that has to be done within the next few hours, but I won't accomplish any of it without a good breakfast to get me going. Right?"

"At the risk of sounding completely inappropriate," Rene said, looking away from Pearl, "it's not like Garnet's going anywhere, is she?"

A broad grin crept onto Pearl's face, and the two of them burst out laughing.

Rene said, "It's so wonderful to see my best friend come back. She hasn't been here emotionally for a long time."

"Feels good to be back," Pearl assured her. "What can I do to help?"

"You can set your rear end down on one of those chairs and talk to me about things we need to catch up on."

"I think I can handle that," Pearl said, pulling a chair away from the table, her voice bright and happy-sounding, and Rene knew a great burden had been lifted from Pearl's heart.

Later that morning Rene went to the grocery store. While sorting through a box of rutabagas, looking for a couple that were the right size for making a rutabaga shepherd's pie, she felt a tap on her shoulder. She turned, and there stood a young woman she'd only seen around town a few times, and always at a distance. "May I help you?" Rene asked.

The young lady said, "Please. Cream. Where?" She had a heavy accent that Rene thought might have been Russian.

"Oh. It's in the cooler behind the checkout counter. You'll have to ask that man for it." Rene pointed to the store owner who was busy adding up the items that Marty, the local filling station attendant, was purchasing.

"Thanking you," the young woman said.

"You're not from around here," Rene said.

"I visit friend," the young woman said.

"How nice. Are you staying long?"

The young woman's face changed from pleasant to aggrieved. "Per…per…"

"Perhaps?" Rene suggested.

The young woman nodded. "Perhaps."

"Well, enjoy your stay."

"Thanking you." The young woman said again, bowing her head, turning, and making her way to the checkout counter.

Rene finished gathering up the items she needed and went to the checkout. The young woman was still waiting in line. "We meet again," Rene said. "I'm Irene, but everyone calls me Rene. May I ask your name?"

"Liliana."

"What a pretty name! Liliana," Rene repeated it. "Are you from Russia?"

Liliana shook her head. "Poland. Warsaw."

"Ahh, that accounts for the accent."

"You visit my country?" the woman asked, the tiniest bit of excitement evident in her voice.

"No. But I like the way your language sounds."

"You talk it?"

"No, sorry. May I be so bold as to inquire about your friend?"

Liliana blinked a few times, obviously not comprehending what Rene had asked.

"Your friend's name. The one you're visiting. I know most of the people who live here. I was just wondering who your friend is."

"My friend...Polly."

Rene thought for a moment, then said, "Oh, Polly Gustavson."

Liliana nodded.

"How did you meet?"

"Skate."

"You both skate?"

"Speed skate. Demonstration sport, Olympics nineteen-hundred thirty-two. I from Poland. Polly, United States. Polly win silver, I win gold, we now friends."

"You won a gold medal in the Olympics?" Rene was overwhelmed.

Liliana shook her head. "Demonstration medal only."

"I don't understand what a demonstration sport or a demonstration medal is," Rene said, hoping Liliana would be able to help her see the light.

"Demonstration sport become new sport next Olympics."

"Oh, I see. But we haven't had the Olympics since 1932 because of the war."

"Sad," Liliana said. "But Polly ask me come to America. Visit."

"How nice!" Rene said. "Do you have a place to practice

your speed skating around here?" She knew there were no ice arenas in Grand Marais.

"Marquette," Liliana said. "Polly take college there. Skate on ice oval. Parents live here, Grand Marais."

"I know her parents. I seem to remember hearing that their daughter was going to travel to Europe several years ago, but I didn't know she was going to be in the Olympics. That's really exciting. And the two of you competed against each other. The world just seems to grow smaller and smaller all the time."

Liliana was nodding, but the blank look on her face suggested that she probably only understood part of what was being said.

"Did I talk too fast?" Rene asked.

Liliana blushed. "Some. But okay. I pay now." She put her groceries on the counter and asked for cream, pointing at the bottle she wanted. When she had finished her transaction, she turned to Rene and said, "We talk again. You most nice," and she left.

Rene decided to make a point of visiting with the Gustavsons. And she thought it might be fun to become acquainted with a person from Poland. Then she remembered that much of Poland had become Nazi-occupied territory and wondered just how bad the situation was near Warsaw. She made a mental note to look into that.

When she got home, she began to put away the groceries, but she jumped when she saw Alvie sitting at the dining room table. It took a moment for her to recognize him in his new state. *That's going to take some getting used to*, she thought. "Hi, Alvie. I ran into someone at the grocery store today who might interest you."

"Liliana," he said.

"How could you possibly know that?" Rene asked him.

He ignored the question and proceeded, purely factual: "Liliana Bartosz of Warsaw, Poland. She competed in the Winter Olympics in February, 1932, in Garmisch-Partenkirchen, a Bavarian ski town in southern Germany. She's currently living with the Gustavsons here in town. Liliana and Polly Gustavson are friends. Liliana won the gold medal in the women's speed skating demonstration sport." He knew Rene wasn't familiar with either demonstration sports or demonstration medals. "The medals look just like the regular Olympic medals, but they're smaller. The demonstration sports are played to promote them for the following Olympics, four years later. But Liliana didn't get to participate in 1936 because…"

"…because the 1936 Olympics were cancelled due to the war. I know," Rene said.

"Here's something I'll bet you *don't* know: Liliana is Jewish." He paused for effect and to allow that fact to sink in. Rene's cheerful expression visibly deteriorated. Alvie continued, "Her parents were sent to a Jewish ghetto in Otwock, Poland, fourteen miles southeast of Warsaw in early 1940, following the Nazi-Soviet invasion of Poland in December of '39." His jaws tightened. "Jews were sent there so their population could be persecuted and exploited." Alvie sounded angry.

"Why was Liliana exempt from being sent there?"

"She wasn't, or wouldn't have been if she'd been there, but her parents were able to have her smuggled out of the country to study at a Russian university in 1938. That was about a year before the ghetto was formed. Her parents knew she'd get an education, be able to practice her speed skating, and probably avoid being captured and disposed of by Hitler's Nazis."

"What is a Nazi ghetto?" Rene asked, softly.

"A neighborhood that's enclosed to isolate Jews from the non-Jewish population and other Jewish communities. There are more than four-hundred ghettos, the majority being in Poland. As you well know, the Nazis view the Jews as an inferior race, and the ghettos have been established to keep them from mixing with and degrading the Aryan race, which is considered superior." His lips pursed, forming a disgusted look. "Where possible, the ghettos are walled off from the rest of the city with gates or barbed-wire fences." He shook his head, dejectedly, then continued. "They're extremely crowded, and the people lack food, water, living space; the conditions are unsanitary. The winter weather has led to repetitious outbreaks of epidemics. And that, of course, leads to high mortality."

Rene couldn't believe what Alvie was telling her. She could hear increasing passion in his voice as he continued.

"But the ghettos are just temporary. In fact, most have only existed for a short amount of time, and already the Germans are destroying them and deporting the Jews to forced-labor camps and extermination camps. And it seems the ghettos have been serving their purpose by making it convenient to exterminate large numbers of the Jewish population." His fists were opening and closing; the more he talked, the faster Alvie balled and opened and re-balled them. He looked Rene square in the face and said, "The ghetto at Otwock was liquidated between August and September of this year."

Rene gasped. "Liliana's parents would have been there."

Alvie's face was red with rage. "About eight-thousand of the Jews who inhabited the ghetto at Otwock were assembled by the Nazis at a layover yard in Otwock and then taken in cattle trucks to extermination camps. Any Jews who were deemed unable to travel—the feeble, the sick, the very old and the very young—were shot! Eight thousand, Irene. And that's from only *one* of the ghettos in existence."

A gray cloud had seemed to settle over Alvie, and it soon enveloped Rene, as well. She hung her head and said, "I understand, now, why you no longer wanted to be Alvie the boy. I might not..." She shook her head and looked deeply into his eyes. "I *would* not have recognized the seriousness of the matter through his carefree, childish demeanor." She felt an intense heaviness in the pit of her stomach, as if a rock had been deposited there. She closed her eyes, hoping to shut out the detailed mural that Alvie had painted on the walls of her imagination, but her effort only made it more vivid, and she silently had to tell herself, *Breathe, Rene.*

She opened her eyes, took some deep breaths, and an unexpected memory of Emmo crossed her mind. He was hitching up the horses in the dark of the early morning. She stood at the kitchen door watching him. He was alternately whistling and talking to Grog and Ivy, and they were chomping at the bit to get going. At that stage in her life, everything had seemed good and right. *Why did it all disappear? Where did it go?*

Alvie was all at once behind her, his hands on her shoulders. "'Tis a fearful thing to love what death can touch. A fearful thing to love, to hope, to dream, to be.'[16]"

1943 - January

CONFUSION AND TRUST

The new year came in without any special observance on Rene's part. "Somehow celebrating at this point in time just seems wrong," she told Alvie. "There is so much local apathy for what's happening worldwide. Unless a family in our town has a service member overseas, they seem oblivious to the whole thing. Do you think people really don't care?"

"I think most of the people here in Grand Marais have a keen awareness about the whole situation. But they realize that being overly concerned may make them unable to cope with their own daily situations right here at home."

"Are you suggesting that I'm *too* concerned?"

"Not at all. You are an exceptional person, Irene. You have a heart that's bigger than most. You're more tuned in—more aware of what's happening—than most of the others, especially since you've seen it firsthand."

Rene pondered that for a moment. "So...I wouldn't be as aware if I hadn't seen it in person?"

Alvie sighed. "Of all the people I've ever guided, you are the most insightful. And Oolanaloo agrees. If Oolanaloo did not have a plan for you, you would not have been granted the opportunity to go where I took you. And without that opportunity, you would have shriveled up and crawled inside yourself, leaving everyone else behind while you were eaten away by sorrow and uncertainty."

"I feel more sorrow and uncertainty now than at any other point in my life. How is that helping me?"

"Trust Oolanaloo."

Rene closed her eyes and tried to accept what Alvie was advising her to do. "Is there some underlying purpose to all of this?" she asked Alvie.

He did not offer a verbal response; he only smiled. And Rene knew she would eventually get her answer.

THE GUSTAVSONS

Between January the first and the thirteenth, it snowed thirty-six inches, common for that part of the country which Rene called home, and it brought the annual snowfall up to one-hundred fifty-four inches, to that point in time. It was, after all, only January, and there were still at least three more months of hard winter to come.

She invited Malcolm, Beatrice, and Polly Gustavson and their houseguest, Liliana Bartosz, for supper. Rene had perfected her rutabaga shepherd's pie, so she served it with yeast rolls and sweet slaw, and she baked a Dutch pudding for dessert. The meal was a hit. "Oh, my goodness, Mrs. Vandersligh. You outdid yourself," Malcolm said, rubbing his belly.

"I absolutely *must* have your sweet slaw recipe," Beatrice said. "I have tried and tried to make it, but I've never been successful. Tell me, is there some secret I'm not aware of?"

"No secret at all," Rene said. "Just be sure you don't skimp on the sugar. I like to add a little bit of grated onion along with the green pepper. And I always make it the night before so it has plenty of time to soak up all the flavors."

Out of nowhere, Malcolm asked, "Do you remember Grange Reiker?"

Rene's eyes lit up. "Of course! He was Emmo's best friend here in town." She paused a moment then said, "I miss Grange."

"Never knew anyone who could quote so many people."

"Oh my, yes. He was never at a loss for a quote if he felt it might be appropriate," Rene answered, a wide grin crossing her face. "What a pleasant memory. I hadn't thought about Grange for some time. Thank you for mentioning him."

They talked about the end of the lumbering era. Malcolm explained that, when he was a very young man, he had worked with Grange at the railroad and was there when Grange had his accident, leaving him without an arm. "Beatrice's father also worked for the railroad. He and Grange were good friends, and it was Grange who suggested to him that he might want to introduce me to his daughter. He did, and you can see the outcome."

"Smart men, those two," Beatrice said, lovingly smiling at Malcolm.

While Rene, Malcolm, and Beatrice continued their polite conversation and sipped some after-dinner coffee, Liliana and Polly left the table to look through a photo album Rene kept on an occasional table in the living room. The album contained ancient photos of Rene's grandparents and parents, a couple of pictures Pearl had taken at Emmo and Rene's wedding, some shots of the ice company in Gulliver, one of the Seul Choix Lighthouse, and several photos of Grand Marais at the turn of the century showing the railroad that Rene so severely missed.

"Tell me about Liliana," Rene said quietly to Beatrice. "Does she know about...about what's going on in her country?"

Beatrice hung her head and uttered a soft mournful noise.

Malcolm said, "Unfortunately, she knows everything about it."

"So, she knows her parents are probably..."

"Yes," Beatrice said, her head snapping up, her eyes roving toward the living room. "We only talk about it if she brings it up."

Malcolm said, "The most difficult part was that the letters from them ceased to arrive after they were locked up in that horrible ghetto. Correspondence simply stopped; no explanation."

"Liliana never got to say goodbye," Beatrice said. She looked straight at Rene, then she closed her eyes, and a single tear crept from beneath her left eyelid.

"Treated like caged animals. The filth must have been unbearable." Malcolm looked off into the distance and shook his head. Both irritation and volume grew in his voice as be continued. "And then carted off to an extermination camp. Goddamned Nazi bastards!" His face turned red, he sucked in a fast breath, and his hand involuntarily jerked up and covered his mouth. "I beg your pardon. I promise you I'm not in the habit of using such language in the presence of ladies."

Beatrice put her hand over her husband's hand on the table. Liliana and Polly appeared at the doorway, a look of pure shock on Polly's face at hearing such an outburst from her father. Liliana's face was blank, distant.

Rene said, "Please don't feel the need to apologize, Malcolm. I admit that I, too, have come incredibly close to such an outburst myself. My respect for you has actually increased because of it."

Malcolm was speechless. Liliana, however, was not. "Nazi scum. Deserve no better. Me, parents, all other Jews think same." She clenched her fists at her sides and shouted in Polish, "HITLER TO DIABEL!" Then she turned and stormed out the front door. Without a word, Polly hurried to the bedroom and retrieved hers and Liliana's coats off the bed and followed her friend.

Rene was horrified. She looked questioningly at Beatrice.

"Hitler is the devil," Beatrice translated.

"I'm so sorry. *So* sorry. How could I have been so unthinking? I had no intentions of bringing up something that would be…could possibly…oh my." Her voice trailed off, and she buried her face in her napkin.

Beatrice tried to soften the moment. "Please don't blame yourself, dear. You must certainly be filled with questions about what is happening on the other side of the world. I assume you don't have anyone who is directly involved. At least, I hope you don't."

It took several seconds for Rene to regain her composure and swallow the large lump that filled her throat. "I don't have anyone directly involved." *Except for Alvie*, she thought. "But I think every person who listens to the radio or reads the news is directly involved…or should be, at any rate. I've often wondered how our town simply goes on, as if no one really cares. Then I think: I care, but what good is my caring? It's not actually helping anyone, is it? And then I think about people like Liliana, and about you and your family, and how you were willing to take in someone who needed you more than…more than I can even imagine. What would she do without you? Her entire world has been shattered." She paused, then she said softly, "Maybe it's more difficult for the living than for those who accepted their fate and summarily met their demise at the hands of the Nazis."

Beatrice's face had paled, and Rene could see that, though she was right there in the room—at the same table—her thoughts were far away.

Rene went on. "Don't get me wrong; I am angry that Japan attacked our naval base in Hawaii, but that was an act of war, not a personal slap in the face to an entire culture. What the Jews have undergone is unspeakable. Barbaric. Ungodly. And here I am, unable to do anything about it. I've been driving myself crazy trying to invent ways to change it all, if given the chance."

Malcolm came to her rescue. "If I may be so bold…it appears that you're suffering from guilt because you cannot personally reverse what has been happening in the world. I say this because Beatrice and Polly and I have all gone through it, as well. When Liliana first came to visit us, we were overjoyed and fascinated at having a connection to a place so far away—one that we could barely identify as a part of our world other than by name and pointing it out on a map." But his voice changed, and the solemnity of the situation became evident when he said, "We were completely unaware of what was on the horizon."

He leaned toward Rene and continued, an almost apologetic tone in his voice. "The world has grown smaller, and its status has deteriorated. You call it a 'slap in the face,' but it is far worse than that. Hitler's actions will leave a terrible scar on this planet, and they will leave an even uglier scar on all of its inhabitants' minds. The three of us—Beatrice, Polly, and myself—agonized over the fact that we were doing *nothing* to reverse it, and each of us finally realized reversing it is impossible for any individual. We must leave the solution to the leaders of our nation and those of our allies."

Malcolm sat back in his chair and looked over at his wife. His voice and his expression changed; there was an obvious tenderness. "Now, however, we feel honored to have been able to provide a tiny bit of comfort to one poor girl who has lost everything dear to her. Everything good that life handed her...taken away." He shook his head.

"Not everything," Rene said. "She still has you."

Malcolm's appearance and attitude changed as if someone had closed a curtain on the subject. He playfully slapped the table with both hands and said, "What say we lighten the mood?"

"I'm all for that," Beatrice added with a sigh of relief.

"Count me in!" Rene said, trying desperately to sound lighthearted. She rose to begin clearing the table, and there, just over Malcolm's shoulder, stood Alvie, giving her a thumbs-up.

THE LAWN OF THE ANFA HOTEL

The Gustavsons took their leave at about 9:00 p.m., and Rene sighed after she closed the door behind them.

Alvie said to her, "You presented them with a wonderful evening."

"You really think so?" she asked, a hint of sarcasm in her voice. "I feel like I may have created some terribly awkward moments."

"On the contrary," Alvie assured her. "You gave them a chance to release some of the pent-up feelings they've been harboring for a long time."

"But Liliana..."

"Liliana, too," he said. "She needed to release her tension just as much as Malcolm did. And you set the stage perfectly."

"Thank you, but I don't look forward to providing that opportunity again in the near future." Rene began running hot water into a dishpan, adding a small amount of powdered dishwashing soap.

Alvie reached up and turned the water off. "Not now," he said.

"But..."

"There are more important things on the agenda at the moment."

"Such as...?"

"We have to make a trip to the Anfa Hotel."

Dar Bagby

Rene's brow furrowed. "Hotel? Where? And why?"

"The Anfa Hotel in Morocco. There are a couple of people there I want you to observe," Alvie said, seemingly unconcerned.

"Morocco? Isn't that in Africa?" She couldn't believe what she had just heard coming from Alvie.

"Yes. Tomorrow is the first day of the Casablanca Conference, and I want you to be there before the actual discussions begin."

"If the conference is tomorrow, why do we need to leave now? We usually just 'pop in' wherever you take me, so..."

"It's already tomorrow there," Alvie said. "Now take my hand, but this time you must remain completely silent. It's not that they can hear us; I just want you to be totally focused on what's going on. If you have any questions, you can ask me when we get back."

Rene put her hands on her head, one on each side just above her ears, as if to keep it from exploding. She closed her eyes and sighed.

"Don't be concerned. You won't experience the emotional overload you did in the past."

"Who am I going to see?" she asked.

"A couple of big-wigs—FDR and Winston Churchill."

Her mouth dropped open, and her eyes grew as big as saucers.

"Now promise me you'll be quiet as a church mouse." He paused. "Irene? Promise me?" He took hold of her hands, removed them from her head, and put them down at her sides. "Promise?"

She nodded, and without having time to blink, right in front of her sat two of the most important people in the world at that moment in time. Both were sitting in chairs on the lawn of the hotel. The President of the United States, Franklin Delano Roosevelt, was wearing a light-colored suit with a dark tie, his legs crossed in a relaxed manner and a wide smile on his face. The Prime Minister of the United Kingdom, Winston Churchill, sat in the other chair. He was wearing a dark suit with a light handkerchief in the left breast pocket, his walking stick propped up against one of his legs, and a light-colored hat with a dark band perched on his left knee. In his right hand was his signature cigar.

Behind them was a hoard of other men; Rene was certain all of them were of some great importance. Most of them were in military uniforms; they appeared to represent several different countries. Rene could only assume they all played a pertinent role in the affairs of the Allied Nations.

Alvie squeezed Rene's hand. She knew it was a reminder to remain quiet and pay attention, even though she was reeling at being in the presence of so much power. It appeared that all of those present were preparing for a photography session. She was right.

A multitude of photos were shot, then all the men disappeared into the hotel except for FDR and Winston Churchill. To Rene's surprise, the two of them began to discuss nothing of importance; they merely engaged in polite conversation. Rene listened to their small talk for a couple of minutes, then Churchill stopped in mid-sentence, raised his head, and looked directly at her. She stiffened.

"What is it?" FDR asked.

"I swear I smell a woman's perfume," Churchill said.

Rene and Alvie were back in Rene's house. "Did he see us? Me?" she asked, nearly in a panic.

"Of course not," Alvie said. "But that's a first for me. I've never taken anyone with me before, and *I'm* not in the habit of wearing women's perfume." He chuckled.

"It's not funny," Rene said, on the verge of anger.

"Of course it is," Alvie said. "Haven't you ever experienced an aroma and not known where it came from? Now you know how it happened."

"Was that the purpose of the trip?" she asked, hardly believing Alvie would take such a risk.

"No," Alvie said. "The purpose was for you to see how closely those two people resemble everyone else in the world. It doesn't matter that FDR and Churchill are so important; they act just like everyone else. They aren't any different than you or any of your friends. It's just that their positions in the world demand that they meet to discuss more globally important matters. But they do it in the same way as you and Pearl or you and the Gustavsons discuss issues."

Rene thought about what Alvie had said, and she began to see the light. "You're right. I've been putting the 'powerful people' up on a pedestal." She reached high above her head. "Way up here. And they aren't any more special than Pearl or Beatrice or…or the checkout man at the grocery store, are they?"

Alvie shook his head and grinned. "Given, what FDR and Churchill are discussing is of the utmost importance to the world," he said, "but as the saying goes, 'They put their pants on one leg at a time, just like you and me.' Well, if you wore pants, that is."

Rene laughed.

"Here's a little story that'll make the point even more poignant. One time Winnie was invited…"

"Wait. Winnie?"

"That's what all of Churchill's personal friends call him."

"And you're a personal friend?"

"Well…no, but I've been around him and his friends a lot without being noticed, so I feel like I know him well enough to call him Winnie. If he knew me, I mean."

"Oh, I see," Rene said, raising her eyebrows.

Alvie ignored her expression and went on. "Winnie was invited to dinner at a prestigious couple's home. The wife noticed that Winnie had finished his roast chicken, and she asked him if he would care for more. 'Yes, I'd like another breast,' Winnie said. The woman blushed and put her napkin to her mouth. 'We refer to it as white meat,' she said.

"The next day a package, addressed to the woman, arrived at the couple's house. She opened the box, and inside was a beautiful orchid corsage with an accompanying note from Winnie. She read the note: 'Dear Madam: Thank you for the wonderful dinner. I hope you enjoy the corsage. I am certain it will look lovely pinned on your white meat.'"

Rene not only laughed, she full-out belly laughed.

When the laughter finally subsided, Alvie filled her in on

the seriousness of what was taking place at the conference. "For the next ten days, they'll be discussing what they're calling 'unconditional surrender' by Germany following the invasions of mainland Europe, Sicily, and Italy, all of which are unavoidable. Two days from now, the RAF—that's England's Royal Air Force—will begin bombing Berlin; that'll last for two nights. And when that ends, there will be an uprising of the Jews in the Warsaw ghetto."

Rene snapped her head toward Alvie. "That's good, isn't it?"

Alvie unceremoniously sunk down onto the kitchen floor and cradled his head in his hands. "I'm sorry. I've said too much. I don't know what got into me. Oolanaloo will be upset if I tell you more before it happens."

Rene blinked, and Alvie was gone.

THE REMAINDER OF THE MONTH

Throughout the rest of January, 1943, Alvie made only brief appearances. Rene knew that the people who were participants in the Jewish resistance in the Warsaw Ghetto in German-occupied Poland[17] needed his guidance far more than she did. But she also sensed that Alvie himself was becoming more and more weary and preoccupied with the oppression, persecution, and suffering being endured by the Jewish population, not only in the extermination camps and ghettos, but all over the world. She could tell he was heavily afflicted by the burden being placed on him, not by Oolanaloo, but by himself. *He takes each problem so personally*, she thought. She knew this to be true because he was not himself during the brief moments he spent with her. In fact, he had, on one occasion, appeared before her as someone she did not know. And when he "came home" to her attic, she heard him pacing for hours on end.

The events which Alvie had said would happen, did. *Why wouldn't they? He's been through them so many times, he knows exactly what to expect.* Rene understood why he had refused to tell her more; not only did she find herself nervously anticipating the events, she also experienced extreme uneasiness at their arrival and the knowledge that there was nothing she, nor anyone else, could do to stop them, or even slow them down. *How does he keep from going insane?*

Following the Warsaw Ghetto Resistance, the Red Army took the last German-occupied airfield at Stalingrad. This provided assurance that the Luftwaffe would no longer be able to supply the German troops, but Hitler demanded that the fighting continue. A surrender to Soviet forces shortly thereafter by the German field marshal, Friedrich Paulus, became the first time a field marshal was captured by the enemy. By the end of the Casablanca Conference, the Allies insisted on Germany's unconditional surrender, and the German forces in Stalingrad entered their final phases of collapse.

On January 27, fifty bombers mounted the first all-American raid against Germany by targeting their large naval base, Wilhelmshaven. On the downside, however, a naval battle near Guadalcanal saw the Japanese beat the Americans, and the USS Chicago *was lost. But on the same date, the RAF launched another two-day bombing of Berlin.*

1943 – February through June

On the second day of February, the German Sixth Army officially surrendered to the Soviet Union following the end of the battle of Stalingrad, and the German public was informed of the action. This marked the first time the Nazis acknowledged a failure in the war effort.

A PLACE TO CALL HOME

On a blustery day at the beginning of February, Rene got out of bed and found Alvie sitting in one of the two overstuffed chairs that faced the fireplace. He was smoking a pipe. "I didn't know you smoked," she said as she settled into the other chair.

"I decided it might make me look more grown-up," he said through teeth clenched around the pipe's stem.

Rene could tell he was trying to suppress a grin. "The tobacco certainly smells nice," she said, "but I don't know how much it adds to your overall façade. Frankly, I found you quite grown-up and attractive before you began smoking."

Alvie reached up and grasped the bowl of the pipe, removing it from his mouth and turning toward Rene, a puzzled expression on his face. "You never said anything about my general appearance other than saying it's pleasant and non-threatening."

She frowned. "As I recall, I never said that aloud."

"I read your thoughts the first time I appeared before you in this body. What makes you think 'attractive' should be added to that?"

"I've always thought you were attractive, both as a nine-year-old boy and as the man you are today." She picked up a magazine that had been lying, unread, on the table separating the two chairs and began thumbing through it. She could both see and feel Alvie's expression change. He seemed to relax, his shoulders and neck easing into a more comfortable position. Rene could feel the tension leaving the room. "You know the government has put a ration on shoes," she said in an off-the-cuff manner.

Alvie went back to puffing away on the pipe, releasing little wisps of smoke with each breath. "Yes, I heard that."

"I'm not sure I understand the reasoning," she said.

"Rubber is needed for the soles of shoes. Now, think about it for a moment. Where is the bulk of the world's rubber produced?"

"I haven't a clue."

"Southeast Asia," Alvie said. "And who controls that area of the world right now?"

"Oh. Japan. Now I understand. But what about leather?"

Alvie started to answer, but Rene said, "No, wait. Don't tell me. Let me think about this for a minute." She wrinkled her forehead and looked off into space. "I guess it's because the military needs it for lots of shoes and boots. Right?"

"Right. And for those leather flight jackets and helmets the airmen wear."

"Huh. There are so many aspects of this war that touch us all, and we're basically oblivious to them until something jars us into the reality of it. I guess I should think about buying only fabric purses and belts instead of leather ones." She turned her attention back to the magazine.

"It's all part of the war effort," Alvie said. "And I have to admit, the United States is really good at supporting it. But 'it only lasts briefly, that feeling of unity, the belief that we're more alike than different, that this nation is not about getting what's good for me, but in finding what's good in all of us.'[18] It's nice to see Americans who are willing to sacrifice for the sake of the country—the world. A lot of countries aren't so eager to do that."

"A lot of countries don't have what we Americans have."

"You're right," Alvie said. "It's no wonder so many people worldwide want to come here to live. Except maybe not so many of them want to live in Grand Marais."

Rene took the comment as an affront. "And what's that supposed to mean?" she asked Alvie. "What's wrong with Grand Marais?"

Alvie burst out laughing. "Not one thing. I just wanted to see if I could get a rise out of you." He continued giggling like the nine-year-old boy he used to be.

"I guess I might be a little over-protective of my home," Rene admitted. She could feel her ears and cheeks warming with an uncontrollable blush.

"I both admire and enjoy your passion about this place," Alvie said, tenderly. "I know a lot of people who've been forced to leave their homeland but still feel the way you do about yours."

Rene considered that for a moment, but she saw the look on his face, and her heart melted. She asked him, "Do you have a place like that?"

"No. I wish I did." He laid the pipe down in a heavy, amber-colored glass ashtray that was sitting on the table between the chairs, then he rose and walked out the front door. Rene hoped he was dressed warm enough for the cold February wind that was blowing outside.

Heavy bombing continued in Nuremberg, Munich, Vienna, and Berlin. On February 9, the American offensive in the Pacific arena achieved its first major victory by securing Guadalcanal, and two days later, General Dwight D. Eisenhower was chosen to command the Allied armies in Europe.

AN EMOTIONAL BREAKTHROUGH

Alvie returned late on the night of February 16. "There's a lot going on right now," he told Rene when she asked if he would be staying for a while. "Have you ever heard of the White Rose Movement?"

Rene looked up at him. "I should know what that is," she said, shaking her head, "but lately I've been concentrating on things around here." She put a small piece of paper in the book she was reading to mark her place, and she lowered the book into her lap. Then she strained to put a smile on her face and turned to Alvie. "Tell me about it."

"You're tired," Alvie said, shaking his head. "We can discuss it another…"

"No," Rene said, cutting him off. "I want to discuss it now. I know you need to vent about all that's going on, and I want to be your sounding board."

Alvie looked deeply into her eyes, a strange expression contorting his face. "Who's the guide here?" he asked quietly. "It's supposed to be me, but you seem to be the one doing the guiding…and consoling." He closed his eyes and released a puff of air through his nose. "I'm sorry if I've been negligent in my duty to you." He opened his eyes, but he quickly averted them from meeting Rene's gaze, and the corners of his mouth turned down.

"Oh, Alvie. I didn't mean to make you feel like you're not succeeding at your task. But it pains me so to see you this sad. You're under a great strain; I know that. And I wish I could just make it all go away." She rose from her chair and sat down on the footstool in front of him. She reached out and took one of his hands in hers, placing her other hand over the top of his. "I need you, Alvie, but I know there are others who are far more desperate for your help, and I don't want to stand in the way of you guiding them."

His gaze slowly met hers. "You're right; I am sad. I've been through this all before—thousands of times—but I never had anyone empathize with me the way you do."

"And that depresses you?" Rene's face contorted questioningly.

"I've known for some time that my purpose in your life has been completed, but deep down inside I've been ignoring it, deliberately denying it. I know I should move on and allow you to get on with your life so you can…"

"Stop!" Rene ordered him. Alvie jumped at her insistence. "Just stop right there! Get on with my life?" she asked. "What do you…can you not see that…that you are a major part of my life now? No, you *are* my life now. I can't 'get on with it' without you, Alvie."

Alvie sighed. "I've been able to read that in your thoughts. I feel things when I'm around you, Irene…things I've never recognized before. Things that sometimes make me dizzy. Things that sometimes embarrass me. Things that even make me wonder if what I'm doing are the things Oolanaloo intends. Sometimes I'm so confused I lose my way when I'm guiding my other subjects. No one, ever, has done to me what you have. You have totally messed with my mind, my heart. I…I'm lost inside myself." He moved forward in his chair, putting his face close to hers. "And I like it," he whispered, "shamelessly."

Rene could hardly breathe. She knew she had avoided admitting to herself that she had fallen in love with Alvie. But she had no idea he had done the same. She had always felt a special bond with him, but now it was evident that he had been struggling with his own emotions about her.

Alvie shook his head. "Suppression is no longer an option."

THE CONTINUING WAR

Joseph Goebbels, the propaganda minister of Germany, declared "Total War" against the Allies on February 18, the same day on which the Nazis arrested prominent members of the White Rose Movement, a non-violent resistance group in the Third Reich led by students who attended the University of Munich. The group's campaign, which consisted of distributing anonymous pamphlets and displaying anonymous graffiti calling for active opposition to the Nazi regime, had begun in June of 1942. It ended on February 18, 1943, however, with arrests; four days later, two members of the movement, Hans and Sophie Scholl, were executed.

Twice during the month of March Rene heard Alvie in the attic, but he did not show his face. Somehow, she knew that keeping his distance was not personal; instead, it was because of his duty to guide lost and suffering individuals through the heinous incidents taking place worldwide. And she loved him all the more for his dedication.

She was once again listening to the newscasts on the radio.

The foreign correspondents spoke of such occurrences as the Battle of the Bismarck Sea where, over the course of three days, naval forces from the U.S. and Australia sank eight Japanese troop transports near New Guinea. There were continued RAF bombings of the Ruhr Valley, especially in Essen. Rommel was forced to retreat following his last battle in Africa. There was a covert attack against a German merchant ship that had been transmitting Allied positions to U-boats. A Greek city was the first to become liberated from Nazi occupation.

Rene was becoming more and more aware of the magnitude of the war. *It truly is a <u>world</u> war,* she thought. In her mind, the most glaring occurrence in March was the liquidation of the Jewish ghetto in Krakow on March 13. She couldn't help but think about Liliana and her roots in Poland. *I know how I would feel if I were in her shoes, if I were "stuck" in a country not my own and were aware of the atrocities taking place in my homeland. I could not simply remain placidly removed from it all, as I know Liliana cannot.*

"It's so good to see you," Rene greeted Alvie, beside herself with joy, but she was met with a tired, lined face and an all-business demeanor.

Alvie did not smile, nor did he make any attempt to discuss pleasantries. "The next few days will be filled with turmoil," he told her. "I will have to be in more places and communicate with more people than I care to think about. So many are depending on me right now. Please be patient, Irene. I think of you nearly every minute of every passing day, but I cannot be with you. Our time will come."

Rene opened her mouth to speak, but Alive disappeared.

Throughout the remainder of April, a large number of German aircraft were shot down during the "Palm Sunday Massacre;" they were on their way to pick up the isolated German troops in Tunisia. The Bermuda Conference, consisting of U.K. and U.S. leaders, was held to discuss the condition of the Jews in Europe. On April 19, the Eve of Passover, the Jews in the Warsaw Ghetto resisted attempts by the Germans to deport the Jewish community. A railway convoy transporting Belgian Jews to Auschwitz was attacked, and two-hundred thirty-six Jews escaped. And on April 30, Operation Mincemeat[19] took place (though Rene was not aware of this particular war tactic at the time).

Dar Bagby

MAYDAY

The townspeople of Grand Marais had become used to ushering in the month of May by having a town-wide Mayday celebration. Most of the businesses found that by offering major sale items, they were able to lure more customers into their stores even though winter still lingered. It gave the business owners a much-needed boost following the notoriously slower months between January and June. But the first half of 1943 had left several of the businesses with no choice but to close their doors. Tourism had dwindled significantly, and many of the inhabitants of Grand Marais were low on cash, leaving the smaller businesses destitute.

"I'm so thankful I was able to sell the Boarding House when I did," Pearl told Rene. They were sitting in the kitchen in Garnet's house; Pearl was not yet able to move back into her own place. She removed a needlepoint cozy from the teapot and refilled Rene's cup.

"It smells so good," Rene said, pulling the tea's aroma up to her nose with her hand, a gesture she had learned from Alvie. "What did you say it's called?"

"Jasmine," Pearl said.

"It sounds so…what's the word I'm looking for?"

"Exotic?" Pearl suggested.

"Yes, that's exactly the word." Rene would normally have added a teaspoon of sugar to her cup, but she had given it up since sugar was being rationed, as were so many other things.

"It feels odd that the town isn't bustling like it used to on Mayday," Pearl said, a hint of longing in her voice.

"It'll come back," Rene said.

"As long as we don't get bombed off the face of the earth," Pearl said.

"Pearl! Don't say such a thing."

"Well, it could happen, you know. We need to face facts."

Rene closed her eyes. "I feel so removed from the facts sometimes. I listen to the radio, and most of what's said sounds like a nightmare to me. I can't imagine those things happening in our country." She opened her eyes, looked at Pearl, and sighed.

"Am I being naïve?"

Pearl shrugged. "Well, the Japanese are still in the western hemisphere, you know. In the Aleutian Islands."

"I guess that *is* North American soil, isn't it?"

Pearl nodded. "Let's change the subject. I can't spend every waking minute of every day thinking about the war, either. But living alone in this big empty house makes that difficult."

"It sure does," Rene said. "I've been truly lonely since…" She stopped short.

"Since what?" Pearl asked.

"Oh, nothing," Rene said, embarrassed that she almost let her thing with Alvie slip out of the bag.

"Come on," Pearl egged her on. "What were you going to say? Out with it. Since what?"

Rene's mind raced. *What can I say to cover up my mistake? It has to sound legitimate.* Then it came to her: "Well, strange as it might sound, it happens every May." She got a faraway look on her face. "May is when I lost Emmo. I always miss him the most in May. I'm glad he's not here to have to face the bad news every day, but at the same time, I still miss him, even after all these years." She hoped her story had been convincing.

Pearl looked down at her cup of tea and remained silent.

"Pearl?" Rene frowned. "Are you okay?"

"I'm sorry. It never crossed my mind that you must miss him so. He's been gone for how many years now?"

"Seventeen." Rene didn't need time to do the math.

Pearl began talking again, but Rene was paying no attention to her friend; she was lost in her own thoughts about Emmo and Alvie. She realized that, for the first time in many days—nearly two months—she was not thinking about the war.

As May disappeared and June showed up on the calendar, the Japanese began to evacuate the Aleutians, their last foothold in the western hemisphere.

Alvie made only brief appearances with little-to-no conversation. Occasionally, Rene could hear him pacing in the attic. It took everything she had to keep from disturbing him.

1943 – July

LILIANA'S HEARTACHE

The first week of July was especially hot for the U.P.: upper eighties/low nineties during the day and dropping only to the upper seventies at night. There was no relieving breeze to speak of, and everyone complained of the heat. People were irritable, short-tempered, ill-humored, and often downright crotchety.

Rene was doing house cleaning and sweating profusely as a result of the weather. Putting away the dishes from the previous night's supper, which she had washed but left out to dry, she dropped a teacup, and it shattered, sending pieces of porcelain all over the floor. She bent over and picked up the biggest of the pieces, slamming them into the sink and creating more shards, smaller and with sharper edges.

She was overcome with tears. *I need an outlet*, she thought. *I miss Alvie so much. I know he's doing his best to help so many others, and I feel ashamed to be craving his company. But I'm not ashamed enough to keep from wishing he were here.* She tossed the dishtowel onto the countertop, ran her fingers through her hair, pushing it away from her face, but it stuck to her forehead for a few seconds and then returned to its irritating position in front of her right eye. She closed her eyes and sighed.

"Anyone home?" a voice called from the back door, which Rene had propped open to let in any stray breeze that might come from across the water. She looked up, and there stood Beatrice Gustavson and Liliana Bartosz.

Rene picked up the dishtowel and wiped her face, hoping the two visitors had not witnessed her erratic act of anger and the tears it provoked. "Hello! It's so good to see you. I'll invite you in in just a minute. I dropped a teacup, and it shattered all over the floor. I don't want you to step on a piece of it." She kneeled and began picking up the smaller pieces.

"We wear shoes," Liliana said. "Not hurt our feet."

"We'll help you clean it up," Beatrice said, opening the screen door and making her way into the kitchen. "We were just coming back from an early morning walk and decided to stop by and see if you were interested in coming to our place for a glass of cold iced tea and some pleasant conversation."

"You couldn't have shown up at a better time," Rene said. "I would *love* to get out of here for a while. It's become like a prison over the last few days. But it's my own fault. I didn't do my spring cleaning while the weather was nice, so I'm paying dearly for it now that it's hot and muggy. And the heat is definitely taking its toll on my disposition."

Beatrice and Liliana reached down and began picking up pieces of the destroyed cup. Rene grabbed the trash can and set it in the middle of the shatter zone. "Thanks for your help," she said after the majority of the pieces had been thrown away. She carefully tiptoed to the corner and retrieved a broom and dustpan, which she used to finish the job. "One of these days I'm going to buy an electric sweeper so I don't have to keep buying brooms that wear out so quickly."

"We have sweeper," Liliana said. "Still wear out brooms."

Rene excused herself and went to the bedroom to change out of her house dress and into something suitable for visiting. She also took time to pin up her hair. When she returned, Beatrice and Liliana were standing at the screen door, fanning themselves and taking advantage of every breath of air that found its way up from the beach. Along with it, however, came the hordes of flies and mosquitoes that always accompanied the suffocating, humid weather at that time of year.

Rene didn't bother closing up and locking the house—no need to in their small town. When they got to the Gustavsons' house, she could see that all the windows and doors were open, and she heard fans running inside. They went in and found Malcolm, who had just come in from doing some of his chores, standing in front of the living room fan, his arms stretched out at his sides, his eyes closed, and his chin raised.

"We have a visitor," Beatrice said.

Malcolm turned to see Rene. He smiled. "Hey! Good to see you. You warm enough?"

"I think so," Rene said. "If not, I'll run back home and grab a sweater."

Malcolm made a terrible face. "Just the suggestion of that makes me sweat worse. Come on in and have a seat. I know there's a pitcher of tea in the kitchen. I'll get us all some."

"I help," Liliana said and followed him to the kitchen.

Beatrice and Rene sat down on the davenport in the direct line of the air moving from the fan. "It would be nice to sit outside, but the bugs are worse than usual this year," Beatrice said.

"That they are," Rene agreed. "I miss going for walks on the beach. The stable flies have hatched out earlier this year than usual."

"Oh, they're the worst," Beatrice agreed. "I've been bitten even up here on the hill. And that's unusual, considering they generally keep pretty much to the beach."

Rene raised her legs straight out in front of her, examining the red, itchy bumps on her shins.

Malcolm entered the room with two glasses of tea, ice tinkling in each one. He handed the first glass to Rene and the second to Beatrice. Condensation was already beginning to form on the outside of both glasses. He returned to the kitchen, passing Liliana on the way. She was carrying two more glasses—one for herself and one for Malcolm. He came back in carrying a plate of shortbread cookies.

With a noticeable amount of disbelief in her voice and a look of horror on her face, Rene asked Beatrice, "You've been baking?"

"Oh, heavens no! Are you kidding?" Beatrice said, taking the plate of cookies from Malcolm. "I bought them at the grocer's yesterday. I wouldn't be caught dead turning that oven on in this heat. It's bad enough just having to warm things up on the stovetop. We've been eating mostly things that don't even need to be cooked."

"That's what I've been doing, too," Rene said. "I have to admit, though, I'm getting a little bit tired of lettuce salad, and cucumbers and tomatoes with vinegar and oil." She took a cookie from the plate and sampled it. "Oh, these are really good," she said after taking a bite. "Who made them?"

"Not local," Liliana said. "Came in large tin from state down."

"Downstate," Malcolm corrected her, smiling.

"Oh, yes. Always say backwards." She blushed.

They discussed things that were happening in town and at church. Eventually, however, their conversation turned to the war. But they kept it very generalized and only discussed its positive aspects.

There was a light rap on the front door, and a man's voice called out, "You in there, Mack?"

"Ya. You ready to tackle that fan belt?"

"Uh-huh."

"Be right out." Malcolm stood, gulped down the remainder of his tea, noisily crunching the ice, and said, "Ladies, it's been nice, but duty calls." He quickly disappeared out the door with the man.

"I think he was glad to leave us," Beatrice said, laughing. "I'm sure he gets a bit tired of hearing girl-talk all the time."

Liliana giggled and said, "Less now since no Polly."

"How is she doing?" Rene asked.

In unison, Liliana and Beatrice said, "Wonderful!"

"She's in Petoskey, right?"

"Yes, and loving it," Beatrice said.

"Hired to big drug store there as chief pharmacol... o... gene...tist," Liliana said, frowning.

Beatrice smiled. "Pharmacologist."

"Yes," Liliana said, rolling her eyes. "Glad for her happiness but miss her."

"I can certainly understand that," Rene said, heaving a deep sigh. "Have you been able to visit her there?"

Liliana grinned and held up her thumb and index finger.

"Two times Mister Papa take me to ferry dock in St. Ignace. I love ferry. Like big boat that bring me to United States." Her expression changed. "Things happy here. Not like Poland."

"*Mister* Papa?" Rene asked.

"That's what she calls Malcolm," Beatrice said.

Liliana explained, "I call him Mr. Gustavson when I first come here. He say, 'Call me Malcolm.' I say, 'No, not proper.' Then he say, 'Call me Papa.' I say, 'But you not my papa. I call you MISTER Papa.' He laugh and say, 'Okay.'" She smiled.

"I like it!" Rene said. It was the longest string of sentences Rene had ever heard from Liliana.

After more pleasant conversation, Liliana glanced at the staircase and said, "I go upstairs now. Must work." She rose, picked up her empty glass, and asked Rene and Beatrice if they wanted more iced tea. Both declined.

"I'm still working on the ice," Rene said. "I'm not about to let it go to waste. What's your current project?" she asked Liliana.

For the past year, Liliana had been doing alterations and making clothing for the locals. Beatrice had told Rene, "I offered her the use of my sewing machine, and she's proven to be a quick learner. People all over town bring things to her now to be repaired or altered, or they ask her to make them new items of clothing."

"I sew now for wedding bridesmaids."

"You mean, a wedding's coming up?"

Liliana nodded.

"Whose, if I may be so bold as to ask?" Rene moved her head back and forth between Liliana and Beatrice.

"Annette Magoteaux," Beatrice answered.

"Yvonne's daughter? Wow! I didn't know she was even old enough to get married."

Liliana answered, "Only sixteen. But Yvonne thrilled because Annette find French boy—man really, twenty-two. Good job. Total dedicated to Annette."

"He's completely smitten," Beatrice said.

"When's the wedding?" Rene asked.

Liliana said, "Middle next month. I make three dress for her. Hard was taking all measurements. Now easy part...to make."

"So we're going to have a wedding in town next month," Rene said. "That'll be the event of the season, don't you think?"

"Without a doubt," Beatrice said, and Liliana smiled, turning to take her glass into the kitchen.

When Liliana returned, Rene asked, "Would it be out of line for me to see the dresses? We wouldn't want to breech proper etiquette, of course, but I'd really like to get a glimpse of what you do."

"I tell no one," Liliana said, grinning. She wiggled her finger at Rene in a come-here gesture, then she turned and started up the stairs.

Rene rose to follow Liliana, then she turned back to Beatrice, who put her finger over her lips, signaling that it was a secret, and a wily smile appeared on Rene's face.

Once in Liliana's room, Rene was pleasantly surprised at how organized everything was. It was almost as if the room had been compartmentalized. The corner to the right of the door contained Liliana's bed and a dressing table. In the opposite corner, between the two corner windows, was a sewing machine—electric, not treadle—and beside it to the right, an adjustable dress form stood on a pedestal. To the left of the machine was a long table that gapped the distance between the sewing machine and the rest of the wall. Behind the door was a clothes rack like one that might be found in a department store; it was loaded with all manner of items from children's clothes to men's shirts to women's dresses and finally the beginnings of what were clearly the bridesmaids' dresses Liliana was currently working on. Rene was impressed.

"This is incredible, Liliana. I had no idea you were so serious about this. There's an entire business going on here. You must be a very talented lady."

"Thanking you," Liliana said, bowing her head slightly.

Rene walked over to the clothes rack and touched one of the bridesmaids' dresses. "Taffeta. Sky-blue taffeta. Beautiful," she said.

"Blue is favorite color to me. Is fun to work on anything this color."

"Oh, Liliana. You have a wonderful set-up here. How could I possibly have been living in this town without knowing how much your business has ballooned? Do you advertise?"

Liliana paused. "You mean, tell people?"

"Yes."

She shrugged her shoulders. "One person like my work, tell other person. I get more work."

"That's called 'word of mouth.' And it's the best kind of advertising you can get," Rene assured her.

"Mister Papa say so, too."

"Well, you can be assured I'll be spreading the word to everyone I know."

"Thanking you…again," Liliana said, lowering her head and blushing.

Rene noticed a small oval frame sitting on Liliana's dressing table. In it was a pale-yellow piece of cloth in the shape of a six-pointed star. An unfamiliar word was embroidered in the middle of the star. Rene recognized the shape as those she had seen on the clothing of the Jews who arrived on the train at the Birkenau station where Alvie had first taken her. She took in a quick breath.

Liliana looked up at Rene and followed her gaze. Then Liliana walked over to the dressing table and picked up the frame, gazing at it longingly. She pressed it to her chest.

"I recognize that symbol," Rene said. "It's the Hebrew Star of David, isn't it?"

Liliana nodded, almost imperceptibly.

"What is the word on it?"

"Shoah," Liliana said, looking off into the distance. "Hebrew word meaning death of Polish Jews." She was noticeably saddened. "But many other Jews die, too: Hungarian, Soviet, German, Romanian, Czechoslovakian…"

Rene could hardly hear Liliana; she was speaking so softly, as if someone who should not hear her, might. "Are you afraid to talk about it aloud, Liliana?"

Liliana shook her head. "No. Make me sad, only. Quiet sadness show respect for dead."

Rene hung her head. "I can't even imagine how bleak it must all seem to you. I know it's selfish of me, but I pray that I will never have to personally undergo sorrow like yours."

Liliana turned her head and looked directly into Rene's eyes. She blinked, and tears welled in her own. "I pray same."

A WHOLE NEW CONCEPT

Walking home from the Gustavsons' house, Rene thought about Alvie. She was aware that he, of course, knew each thing that would happen worldwide during the remainder of the war. But Liliana's personal struggle with her own heartache only served to remind Rene that she would continue to witness the pain coursing through Alvie as each event occurred. She knew he was responsible for guiding people through emotions brought on by the atrocities that always accompany war, and she hoped that Liliana had someone like him to help her. Nevertheless, she promised herself she would do her best to keep him distracted with other, more pleasant, topics.

When she got back home, Alvie was there, waiting for her. He took her in his arms and held her tightly against himself, swinging slowly from side to side. "I have missed you more than I have ever missed anyone before," he said. "It has been absolute torture not being able to spend time with you. Just let me hang onto you so I know you're really here in my arms at last."

Rene was speechless. She had no idea how to interpret the passion Alvie was expressing. *Is it just that he needs to be comforted? Does he need simple companionship? Or does he crave reassurance? Security? What is it that he needs?*

"All of that," he whispered into her ear. "And more."

Rene dropped her arms from around him, but he picked them up and put them back. "Please, please keep holding me."

She squeezed him tighter. "I will hold you forever if that's what it takes to comfort you."

He said nothing, but Rene knew—could feel—that their mere physical contact was easing Alvie's troubled mind. They remained there, embracing one another for several minutes. Nothing was said. Nothing needed to be said.

At last, Alvie released his clutch, though he did not let her go altogether; he kept one arm around her waist. She knew he sought tangible support, so she allowed him to cling to her as long as it might take for him to overcome his obvious lack of security and his longing to be physical, to feel her, not just be near her. She tried hard not to think about anything that could possibly upset him because she knew he could read every one of her thoughts. Eventually, he let her go.

They looked into each other's eyes; there was so much unspoken communication between them. In his eyes Rene saw the answers to questions she had been asking for years. The two of them were understanding each other on a subconscious level, and a whole new connection was becoming apparent. She no longer had to imagine the sensations Alvie had been experiencing; they were all evident without the need for him to speak of them. Every tiny nuance of expression was right there in his eyes.

She was bowled over with awareness, with a newfound recognition of what had been going on for so long; she was finally aware of what Alvie had meant when he told her Oolanaloo wanted her to "understand." She became lightheaded and felt herself nearly losing consciousness. Alvie kept her from fainting by holding her and telling her how proud he was of her for finally accepting her feelings and openly sharing them with him.

But Rene was a realist. "We can't let this happen. I won't be able to cope with not being near you when you're hurting so desperately inside with every subject you guide. How can I handle my feelings now that I'll be troubled by a constant, irreparable ache when we're apart? How can I cope with my own torment?"

Alvie let go of her and backed away. He tilted his head slightly to one side and smiled. "We will not be apart."

She looked at him with blatant confusion. "How can that be? I'll be here, and you'll be…anywhere…and probably experiencing some other timeframe. How can we not be together and still be in contact with one another?"

"I'll only be in one place," Alvie said, "if you and Grand Marais and Lake Superior will accept me."

Rene felt her mind rushing a thousand different directions at once. Her thoughts were jumbled, disassociated from one another, and her insides were jumping and twitching. She tried to speak, but no sound came out.

Alvie said, softly, "I have spent hours-upon-hours communicating with Oolanaloo. We agree that my time is now meant to be spent with you. *All* of my time."

Rene began panting. "I don't understand. You mean you won't be leaving? Ever again? Oh my! Oh, Alvie!"

He took her face in his hands. "Close your eyes and take some deep breaths."

But she was afraid to blink, let alone close her eyes completely for fear that he'd disappear.

He said calmly, "I will not leave you. I convinced Oolanaloo to let me be a part of what's going on in your life, your world, not just be a visitor here; that's a huge difference." He removed his hands from her face and stepped back.

How can he be so calm at a time like this? How can he expect <u>me</u> to be calm at a time like this? But as she began breathing, shallowly at first, then deeper and deeper, her composure began to return.

"That's much better," Alvie said. He moved back toward her and once again took her in his arms.

Rene allowed herself to be supported by his loving grasp. "All right," she said. "You need to do some explaining. I don't fully understand what just happened." She was sweating profusely, not only from the heat but also from the intensity of the moment. Her hair was wet, and her blouse was soaked through. "Oh, I need some air," she said, panting and pushing away from him. She used her sleeve to wipe the perspiration from her face and neck, and at the same time, she kicked off her shoes and stood, barefoot, on the cool floor. She unbuttoned the top two buttons of her blouse then untucked it from her skirt, pulled it out away from her body, and blew down into it, fanning it back and forth, moving the air around her torso. "Take me someplace nice and cool," she said to Alvie, reaching out and grasping his hand. But they remained right there in her kitchen.

At first, Rene thought Alvie hadn't heard her request.

"I heard you loud and clear," he said. "But I can't do anything about it. My travel time is over."

She was still clueless as to what he truly meant. "You mean, you won't be guiding any subjects ever again?"

"That's right."

"You won't be disappearing and reappearing at the drop of a hat?"

"I won't."

"You'll be living someplace other than in my attic?"

He laughed.

"You're going to be staying in one place? Here? In Grand Marais?"

He tilted his head and smiled.

"And Oolanaloo is okay with that?"

"It's at Oolanaloo's command."

She looked around. "Are you visible to everyone now? Not just me?"

He nodded.

Again, Rene was short of breath. "We have to discuss some things. Make some plans. We can't just suddenly appear together. In front of everybody. It doesn't work like that with humans. We have to take other people's perceptions of this into consideration. We need to…"

Alvie was laughing out loud. "Breathe, Irene."

THE PLAN

"Are you still immortal?" Rene asked.

"Yes," Alvie said.

She frowned. "So you won't age like all the rest of us?"

"Oolanaloo will see to it that my appearance changes with time, if necessary. But I'll live right here on this planet, on a day-to-day basis, just like you and all other humans before you."

Rene took a moment to digest that fact. Here was a man who had existed since time began, had been places no one even knew existed, had met and associated with beings completely foreign to human imagination, and now he was willing to leave it all behind…for her. She closed her eyes and covered her face with her hands, as if that act would somehow cause her confusion to dissipate. "But you don't have the same memories as other humans. You don't have parents, right?"

"That's right, but I look to Oolanaloo as a mother/father-figure. Oolanaloo has always been my source for guidance."

Rene smiled. "Did Oolanaloo finally endow you with some fashion sense?"

Alvie chuckled, seemingly glad that she had chosen to lighten the mood. "Well, that's one deficit you'll be somewhat responsible for correcting. May I depend on you to keep me from looking…um, unfavorable?"

Rene's smile broke into an all-out grin. *I like the idea that he's already making it obvious he needs me.*

"More than you can imagine," he said.

"I guess that means Oolanaloo allowed you keep your ability to read minds?"

"Only yours."

"And you'll be eating regular food now, too?"

Alvie's face lit up. "I hadn't thought about that. This opens up a whole new world for me, doesn't it?"

"I have an idea," Rene said. "You go sit down at the table, and I'll fix you something." She knew he'd read her mind, so it was no secret, what she planned to fix, but that didn't matter to her. She took out a pan, put a bit of popcorn into it, placed a lid over the top and set it on the stove. As it began to heat up, she started to wiggle the pan back and forth to keep the kernels moving so they wouldn't burn. When there were no more pops, she took it off the stove and dumped it into a large bowl. Then she used the hot pan to melt some butter, which she poured over the white, fluffy treat, and she sprinkled it with salt.

"I hope it tastes as good as it smells," Alvie said. They nibbled at the popcorn as they continued to devise a plan.

"First off," Rene said, "you'll need to appear as a stranger in town. We can't let anyone know we're already acquainted."

Alvie frowned.

"If you just suddenly show up at my house, it will destroy my reputation as a well respected woman," Rene said.

"'You should be more concerned with your character than your reputation, because your character is what you really are, while your reputation is merely what others think you are.'[20]"

"You're absolutely right, Alvie, but it's important not to let this whole thing get blown out of proportion. There would be too many unanswerable questions. Okay?"

He nodded. "How about if I stay hidden here until dark, then you can drive me out of town and drop me off where no one can see. I'll stay out in the woods overnight…"

"You can't do that!"

"Why not? I'm sure I've been in far worse situations."

Rene was beside herself with worry. "The weather. The animals. The bugs!"

"Can't think of a better way to begin my life as a human," Alvie said, apparently unconcerned. "When the sun comes up, I'll just walk into town with my valise—do you have one I can borrow?"

She scratched her head and sighed. "I have a big oilcloth bag; it was Emmo's. I used it to bring my coats and heavy clothes here when I moved up from Gulliver. I'll give you a couple of blankets for the night—one to lie on and one for a cover. You can stuff them into the bag so it looks like you're carrying your goods with you. You'll have to appear as a foot-traveler. No. As someone who's been thumbing his way from…uh…from out west. Iron Mountain, maybe. Do you know anything about Iron Mountain?"

Alvie sighed. "No. I don't really know any of the particulars about anywhere around here except Grand Marais."

"Rats! Okay, you'll have to be from a place I'm familiar with so I can fill you in. Or better yet, maybe you should be from a place so far away, no one here in town will be familiar with it. You can talk about it without anyone being the wiser."

"Another country?"

"That's a good idea," Rene agreed. "Alaska! They speak

English there, so you won't need to remember to speak with an accent. And I can guarantee you that no one here in Grand Marais has ever visited Alaska."

Alvie laughed. "Not exactly another country." His smile disappeared, and he sighed. "This could be difficult."

"Welcome to being human."

After a couple more hours of discussing the plan and arriving at final conclusions, Alvie sat back, laced his fingers together, and asked, "Is there any more popcorn?"

Throughout July, Hamburg, Germany, was bombed by what was, at the time, the heaviest assault in the history of aviation; it was called "Operation Gomorrah."

1943 – To the End of the Year

A WELL-KEPT SECRET

The plan went exactly as anticipated. The stranger known as Alvie Wybel became a familiar face around Grand Marais. He was friendly and well-liked by everyone he met. He was staying at Bertrand Tinker's house, the man who did the cleaning at the Lutheran church—Rene's church—on the edge of town. Bertrand was elderly and had become increasingly feeble; he had trouble completing some of the physically demanding work, so Alvie had volunteered to help him, and Bertrand soon turned the job over to Alvie. It didn't pay much, but Alvie didn't care. He and the minister hit it off immediately; they spent many hours discussing religious issues, which was right up Alvie's alley. And it was the church where Alvie "met" Irene Vandersligh.

Pearl had become close with Richard Houghton, one of the men who tended the Coast Guard station. Pearl was thrilled to see Rene so happy, and the two of them spent hours together talking about their newfound male friends. One Sunday after the church service, Rene was waiting for Alvie to finish policing the sanctuary, then he, Rene, and Richard were going to Pearl's for Sunday dinner. Pearl whispered to Rene, "Isn't it great having a man around?"

"I can't tell you how good it feels," Rene whispered back. She felt like a schoolgirl whispering and giggling about boys with her best friend.

"I'm going to run along home and finish up in the kitchen," Pearl said. "You and Alvie can come over as soon as he's finished."

"What about Richard?" Rene asked.

"He has to work until twelve-thirty, then he's free for the rest of the day. I'm planning to eat about one, right after he gets there."

"Do you need me to come along and help? I can just tell Alvie I'm going with you now, and he can come when he's finished," Rene suggested.

"Thanks, but not necessary. I have everything taken care of. I just want to make sure it's all hot when we're ready to eat. Oh…" she snapped her fingers. "I almost forgot. I need to put the rolls in the oven."

"Okay. See you in about half an hour."

The heat of July had finally departed, and though August was now upon them, there were many days when the temperature didn't climb above the mid-sixties, and the nights remained in the lower fifties. The usual breeze from off the water prevailed and was, overall, quite pleasant.

Pearl had put Garnet's big house up for sale and moved back into her own little bungalow following the completion of the cabin court on the site where her boarding house had once stood. She had considered the possibility of keeping Garnet's place and selling her small one, but she decided the bungalow was a perfect size for her.

As Alvie and Rene were walking to Pearl's place, Alvie said to Rene, "I'm amazed at how many social events take place over the consumption of food. You Americans really do concentrate on making a meal the center of entertaining, don't you."

"You mean it's not that way around the rest of the world?"

"Well, to some degree, yes, but here it's almost like a full belly's a precursor to having a good time," Alvie said, laughing.

Rene smiled. "You have to remember that we don't have a whole lot of entertainment options in this little town. I mean, we don't even have a theater or a civic center like bigger cities have."

"You have bars," Alvie said.

Rene gave him a look that suggested his statement was nonsense. "Most women don't want to be seen very often in those kinds of places."

"Why not?"

"They give a woman a bad reputation," Rene said, confused over the fact that he didn't seem to know that.

"But didn't you say Pearl had a really nice bar at her boarding house?"

"Yes, but it was mostly visited by her boarders, Alvie, not the locals."

"I don't get it," Alvie said. "What makes the difference?"

"You must certainly understand that, when consumed in excess, alcohol can make people do crazy things."

"Yeah, I understand that. I guided a lot of drunks and alcoholics. But what about the people who just like to get together and socialize? Isn't a bar the perfect place to do that?"

Rene paused and heaved a loud sigh. "How can I put this? You know, a minority often provides the basis for the opinions of the majority."

"I thought you always relied on actions, not opinions," Alvie said.

"I do. But a lot of people think that because a few bar patrons take advantage of the alcohol, then *all* patrons must do the same. Some people even feel that the consumption of any alcohol at all is a sin, you know."

Alvie's face contorted, and he shook his head. "I'll never understand the fickleness of the human mind."

"Not very many people do, myself included."

They had arrived at Pearl's, so the conversation was tabled.

Following a delightful meal of Swiss steak, mashed potatoes and gravy, creamed corn, and Pearl's cloverleaf rolls, they all decided it would be best to let dinner digest before indulging in dessert. Pearl suggested playing charades.

"I'd love it!" Rene said. "We haven't played that for a long time. What say you, Alvie? Wouldn't you like to play?"

"I never have," Alvie said.

Richard piped up, grinning, "You've never played, or you've never *liked* playing?"

Pearl and Rene laughed. Alvie didn't appear to be sure how to answer that. His face reddened, and he said, "Uh, the former."

"It's a fun game, Alvie. I think you'll get a kick out of it," Pearl assured him. "Gals against guys."

They taught Alvie the particulars, and it turned out to be the perfect game for him. Rene was pleasantly surprised at his ability to come up with the necessary pantomimes to provide answers. He was so good at it, in fact, the guys won.

They had returned to the table and were eating peach cobbler when Pearl asked Alvie, "Where did you ever learn so much about literature and art and music?" She was pouring coffee for all of them.

"I have my sources," Alvie said teasingly and winking at Rene.

"Don't let him fool you," Rene said. "He knows a whole lot more than he lets on." Of course, only she and Alvie knew the real story behind the wink.

Bertrand had closed up his house (after offering it for sale to Alvie and Alvie politely turning him down) and had moved in with his brother and sister-in-law in Escanaba, so Alvie was sleeping in the storage building behind the church where all the maintenance equipment was kept. The minister had provided a cot and a folding chair. He also gave Alvie a lamp and a bookcase that weren't needed in the church office. The bookcase provided a place for Alvie to keep his clothes and other personal belongings. He used the bathroom inside the church (and that's where he learned to shave—a new experience for him). He bought a hot plate that he kept on his bookshelf to warm up food. Pearl gave him an old radio from Garnet's house, and Rene supplied his bed linens, including a pillow and a quilt.

Rene was curious about his living conditions, but she knew she didn't dare be seen going in or out of the building. Alvie did his best to describe it all to her. He was excited to have such lavish accommodations. "After all, I've been used to living in an attic," he told her with a grin.

THE WORLD OUTSIDE GRAND MARAIS
When their camp at Auschwitz was liquidated, 2,897 Romani were gassed. Polish Jews began resistance with minimal weapons in Bia-

lystok, and the leaders committed suicide when they ran out of ammunition.

By the time September arrived, 22,750,000 British men and women were in service doing "essential war work." Italy dropped out of the war, and Eisenhower publicly announced the Italians' surrender to the Allies. Nazi Germany began the evacuation of civilians from Berlin. Iran declared war on Germany.

In October, the Sobibor Extermination Camp Underground, led by Polish-Jewish POW Alexander Pechersky, covertly killed eleven German SS officers and several camp guards, though their plan had been to kill all of the SS and walk out of the camp's main gate; however, the killings were discovered, and the inmates ran for their lives while under fire. But about half of the six-hundred prisoners escaped into the surrounding forests.

In November alone, approximately 43,000 Jews were shot at three camps in Poland in what was referred to as a two-day "Harvest Festival." On November 15, German SS leader Heinrich Himmler ordered gypsies and part-gypsies to be put on the same level as Jews, and he placed them in concentration camps. Prisoners of the Janowska concentration camp staged a massive escape when ordered to cover up evidence of a mass murder; most were rounded up and killed. Heavy bombing of Berlin continued. FDR, Churchill, and Stalin established an agreement concerning an offensive on Europe to be accomplished in June of 1944, codenamed "Operation Overlord" (the invasion of Normandy).

THE GALES OF NOVEMBER

The fall colors in Grand Marais usually peaked in either the last week of September or the first week of October, and 1943 was no different except that, for some reason, Rene and most of the others in town thought the colors were brighter than usual. A lot of people said the hard freeze during the third week of September probably had something to do with it; people were always trying to figure out why one year might be different from the next. But Alvie knew the real reason was that Oolanaloo had made it happen for the sole purpose of providing something pleasant to divert Grand Marais's attention from the war.

The fierceness of November was in direct opposition to the serene beauty of the passing of October. Lake Superior, because of its enormous expanse, is capable of creating its own weather. Often, especially in November, that weather comes about startlingly fast. A light breeze turns into a gale-force wind in a matter of minutes, the whitecaps and swells increase in size quicker than calculated, torrents of rain pour forth from clouds that darken and split open in less time than a boat full of fishermen can reckon, swamping it and driving it unmercifully under the surface. Those who live to tell about Superior's storms firsthand are the few and the lucky.

All of Grand Marais was taken by surprise when a horrible storm came heaving and pitching out of the northwest in less than ten minutes on the morning of November 14. The skies turned from pale blue to dark gray and boiled relentlessly as Rene and Alvie watched, silently, through the window over Rene's kitchen sink. Cold, unbearable, torrential rain and lake spray pelted every surface in sheets that blew horizontally. The sound of the pounding surf that had not been noticeable one minute was deafening the next.

All the inhabitants of Lake Superior's southern shore cringed, and the families of every fisherman were silent with fear. Superior, Rene's lake, revealed her severity on that day, claiming the lives of seven Grand Marais fishermen. Three days after the storm, two bodies washed ashore; the other five would spend eternity in the lake's dark, cold-water crypt.

Following the burial service for the two men whose bodies had been recovered, a memorial service was spoken for the five who had not surfaced. Every resident of the town capable of finding a way to get to the cemetery was present. A wooden marker bearing the names of the five missing fishermen was erected between the graves of those who had been buried that day, and beneath those five names were these words:

These bodies lie not beneath the soil.
They rest, instead, 'neath waves that roil

Above the floor of the greatest lake.
Superior gives, but she's ne'er loath to take.

A CHRISTMAS EVE SURPRISE
In December, General Dwight D. Eisenhower became the Supreme Allied Commander in Europe and was officially named head of "Operation Overlord."

On December 10, a snowstorm left behind about eighteen inches of white. Two weeks later, Rene, Alvie, and Richard spent Christmas Eve day at Pearl's house. Ruby and Reese came up from Manistique, and Opal came up from St. Ignace with a man from the bank where she worked. Ruby and Opal both seemed to approve of Alvie.

It was an effort to squeeze all eight people into Pearl's little house, but as Ruby put it in her usual bubbly style, "It just makes things cozier, don't you think? This is the way Christmas should be."

They had all agreed not to exchange gifts. Instead, they each pledged to donate some hours of community service for the war effort during the week between Christmas and the new year. They were, surprisingly, entertained by Christmas carolers (members of the Lutheran church choir) at Pearl's door. Pearl said, "I'd invite you all in for coffee, but I don't know where I'd put you!"

It all made for a joyous day.

Ruby and Reese, and Opal and her friend left early so they could get back home before it got too late. Reese had drawn the short straw at the police station and was on duty for Christmas day, which, for him, began at four-thirty a.m. Opal decided she'd like to get started back to St. Ignace before dark since the roads might get slick as the sun and the temperature went down, but everyone figured she and her friend probably had a "thing" going on and wanted to spend time alone. So Rene and Pearl cleared the table and did the dishes while Alvie and Richard disappeared outside. When the two men came back in, they both had a suspicious look on their faces.

"What's going on with you two?" Rene asked from the kitchen, drying her hands on a dishtowel. She figured they were up to no good. Pearl put the last of the dishes in the cupboard beside the sink, then she and Rene collapsed onto the small settee in the living room.

The two men looked at each other, and Alvie stepped back, giving an exaggerated motion toward Richard. Richard cleared his throat and said, "Please forgive me for not following the decision of the crowd, but I have a gift for the woman with whom I've been spending so much enjoyable time." He walked up to Pearl and knelt before her. He put his left hand out toward her, knuckles up, fist closed.

Pearl looked at Richard's hand, then she looked over at Rene, who shrugged. Pearl's gaze continued up to Alvie, who was grinning from ear to ear. She reached for Richard's left hand, and he turned his fist over and opened it; it contained a small box. Pearl gasped; she sat there, stark still, looking at what Richard was holding.

"Are you going to take it?" Richard asked.

Pearl's gaze was fixed on the box. She didn't move. She didn't speak.

"Well?" Richard pushed it toward her.

She finally swallowed and looked up at him. He smiled lovingly at her. She reached for the box, but he quickly closed his fist and retracted his hand. "Uh-oh. Time's up. You waited too long," he teased, snatching the box away.

The exasperation on Pearl's face was indescribable, and without warning, she shoved him hard enough to knock him off his knee and into a sitting position on the floor.

Pearl regained her composure and said, "I was just taking a little time to gather my thoughts."

"And just *what thoughts* were you thinking?" Richard asked.

She paused for a few seconds before saying, "I was thinking that I don't really know what's in that box. It could be anything from A to Z. I don't want to react inappropriately when I open it, so I was preparing myself for a surprise."

"It's no surprise," Richard said. "It's exactly what you're

thinking it is. What you're *hoping* it is." He raised the box back up to her in his left hand, and with his right hand, he opened the box, exposing a diamond engagement ring.

Hardly able to breathe, Pearl said, "It *is* exactly what I was thinking…*hoping* it would be."

Richard took the ring from the box and placed it on her left ring finger. "Pearl, will you…"

But before he could finish, Pearl said, "Yes, I will, and I'm guessing that answer is exactly what *you* were *hoping* it would be."

1944

AN UNNERVING CONVERSATION

Rene and Alvie had just finished lunch and were sitting at the table allowing their meal to digest. Rene said, "I'm a little bit confused about something."

"What's that?" Alvie asked.

"I don't understand the difference between the Red Army and the Bolsheviks. Are they the same, or no? And I'm not sure if Oolanaloo left you enough memory to be able to explain it."

Alvie put his head down, took in a deep breath, and let it out slowly. He appeared to Rene to be trying to figure out how to answer her question. He looked up at her. "I have memories of the entire war, Irene. I can recall everything about it, just as you would if you were, say, a foreign war correspondent. And I remember all the places I have *ever* visited, not just the ones during the war. Thanks to Oolanaloo, however, I don't have the ability to recall all of the subjects I guided or their problems, which eases my mind by not having to rehash all of *those* details."

"Oh. I didn't realize how much you'd be able to remember. Now that I think about it, that makes good sense."

"Why have you not asked me about my memory until now?" Alvie asked.

She shrugged. "I figured it was a sensitive subject, and you'd bring it up when you were ready. So, I just sort of avoided it."

Alvie looked lovingly at her. "That's so thoughtful. I'm about ninety-nine-point-nine percent sure most other people would pester me constantly about everything I've seen and done."

"I would never do that," Rene said, seriously. "I'm aware that what your past encompasses is far beyond my comprehension, anyway, so why bring up things I wouldn't even understand."

Alvie was smiling at her, unmistakable love written all over his face. He set his water glass down, not taking his eyes off her, and reached across the table, placing a hand on hers. "Of all the memories I have, you and our life together are, by far, the most enjoyable. I'm so glad Oolanaloo chose to allow me to keep those memories."

"But I was a wreck for a long time, and you helped me through it all, just like I'm sure you did for so many others. Why would Oolanaloo allow *my* problems to remain in your memory?"

Alvie looked away for a moment, as if he were gazing into a different time and place. When he finally spoke, his voice was distant, softer, almost unfamiliar to Rene. "Without those memories, I would not know you, Irene. And I made it perfectly clear to Oolanaloo that the only personal thing I truly want to remember is our life together. Not your life before we met; whatever memories you harbor are yours to keep for your lifetime, but mine had to be filtered. So I chose only to remember what has happened to us since I came into your life." He chuckled and looked back at her, "…as bizarre as that episode was."

Rene grinned. "Yeah, I don't recall ever talking to another woman who fell in love with a man who was living in her attic."

"In answer to your initial question…"

Rene frowned. "Oh, you mean about the Red Army and the Bolsheviks."

"Uh-huh. How in-depth do you want me to go?"

"I have nothing planned for the rest of the day," she teased, smiling.

"Okay! I love talking about all of this stuff," Alvie said, settling back in his chair, rubbing his hands together. "But it's gonna cost you a cup of coffee."

Rene stood up, went to the stove, and turned up the burner under the percolator to reheat the already-made coffee. She puttered around in the kitchen, and when the coffee was hot, she took the pot to the table, poured Alvie and herself a cup, then set the pot on a potholder. She sat back down, laced her fingers together in front of her, and said, "I'm ready if you are. And you know I love listening to your explanations about things just as much as you love talking about them."

Alvie scratched his head. "Well, back in 1898, there was a Marxist group called the Russian Social Democratic Labor Party—the RSDLP—a socialist political party who had a faction called the Mensheviks. Two of its party members, Vladimir Lenin and Alexander Bogdanov, split from the Menshevik faction and formed their own party in 1912. It was a far-left, radical, revolutionary party called the Bolsheviks, which is Russian for 'majority.' The Russian word is *bolshinstvo*."

Rene was already completely wrapped up in what he was telling her.

"The Bolsheviks took power in 1917 when they overthrew the provisional government during a revolution in October of that year, and they became the only ruling party in Soviet Russia; they considered themselves the leaders of the revolutionary Russian proletariat. The Red Army was formed in 1918 as the military force of the Bolshevik regime, and their purpose was to defend that new regime during the Russian Civil War."

Rene asked, "But why did they choose the name 'Red Army'?"

"Great question," Alvie said. "*Krasnaya Armiya* is the Russian term for the Russian National Military Forces, also known as the RKKA, and it refers to the color red, which symbolized the blood shed by the workers and peasants in their struggles against oppression."

"So, the Red Army still exists and is the same faction that's fighting in our current war?" Rene asked.

"Big time!" Alvie said.

Rene's brow furrowed, obviously unfamiliar with his comment.

Alvie rolled his eyes. "That's an expression you'll hear in the not-too-distant future," Alvie said. "It seems Oolanaloo allowed me to retain the portion of my vocabulary that hasn't become popular yet."

Rene merely shook her head.

"Anyway, back in June of 1941, when the Nazi assault took place on the Soviets, the Red Army had almost five million troops!"

"Makes you glad they're on our side, huh?" Rene said.

"Well..." Alvie seemed unsure about that.

"What do you know that you're not telling me?" Rene asked.

Alvie frowned. "I'm not sure. There's just something about the whole Soviet system that bothers me. I mean, I know Russia is our ally against the Axis powers, but somewhere down deep inside me, I'm concerned about our relationship with the Soviets. Seems to me that there's a..." he rubbed his forehead, "...a tension, I guess, because of the way Stalin rules his country. Strikes me as almost tyrannical, the communism and all."

Rene spoke up. "I'll admit, I don't understand the whole thing as well as you, but I don't believe there's as much of a problem as you may think. I'll also admit that I'm kind of emotional about some things concerning the Soviets, and Liliana Bartosz's family is one of those things. I think it was wonderful that the Soviets reestablished their diplomatic relations with Poland shortly after the start of the war. That has to be important for the lives of all the Polish Jews. Isn't it?"

Alvie paused...a long pause. "The Soviets broke off talks again just last year after the Polish government demanded the examination of the Katyn Massacre."[21]

"The what?" Rene asked.

"You know about that, don't you?"

Rene was a bit embarrassed. She uttered a sound that was part sigh, part groan. "I guess not. It must have happened during the time period where I simply quit listening to the news because I was so tired of all the negative reports." She clutched the back of her neck and rubbed it, slowly rotating her head back and forth as if to keep it from freezing in one position. She emitted an enormous sigh. "My brain was threatening to shut down, and I wasn't going to let that happen."

"Do you *want* to know about it?" Alvie asked.

She closed her eyes. "Not right now. We'll have other opportunities to talk about that."

"Absolutely," Alvie assured her. "I just want you to keep in mind that even Winston Churchill said, "The Bolsheviks can be very cruel."

THE FAREWELL

The phone rang, and Rene answered it cheerily. The voice on the other end of the line was not so cheery, however. It was Pearl.

"What's up? You sound down-in-the-dumps," Rene said.

"Can you come over?"

"When?"

"Now," Pearl said.

Rene thought it sounded as if Pearl might be crying. "Of course. I'll be right there." Rene's brain was flooded with questions and possible scenarios. Alvie was at the church to help set up tables in the fellowship hall for a benefit dinner the ladies' group was having for a local family whose bread winner had fallen off the roof while shoveling snow and was now laid up with a broken back. Rene decided to stop at the church and explain to Alvie that she had no idea how long she'd be at Pearl's, and she didn't want him to end up running all over town trying to find her.

When she got to Pearl's house, Pearl was waiting for her at the door. The sight of Rene made Pearl's face scrunch up in a terrible contortion, and tears poured from her eyes.

"Oh, Pearl! What's wrong?" Rene hurried to embrace her friend, who buried her face in Rene's coat and wrapped her arms around Rene's waist. Rene was hoping nothing was wrong with her or Richard or Ruby or Opal.

"We only have a couple of months before the wedding, and now I'm not going to be able to have it," Pearl said between sobs.

Rene's mouth flew open. "You mean you're not getting married? What happened? What did Richard do? Has he called it off?"

"No, no," Pearl said, backing away from Rene and uselessly trying to dry her eyes on the sleeves of her housecoat. "It's not that. We're still going to get married; we just won't be able to have the wedding here." She looked up at Rene, and the waterfall of tears began again.

"Then where?"

"Maine," Pearl squeaked.

"Maine!"

"Richard just got word that he's being transferred to a Coast Guard station there. Someplace called Southwest Harbor. It's on an island. An island! It's so far away, I'll never see you again."

"One step at a time, Pearl. Let's just take this one step at a time," Rene said, trying desperately to be positive when, in fact, she wanted to join Pearl in crying about the whole thing. "Let me get my coat off, then we'll sit down and talk about it."

"Oh, of course," Pearl said, embarrassment showing on her face. "I'm sorry. I'm just so…so…"

"I'm sure you are," Rene suggested. "Didn't Richard have any previous warning about being relocated?"

"None," Pearl said, hanging Rene's coat on a hook beside the door and putting her hat and gloves on the bench where Rene sat down to remove her boots. "It came as a total shock. Come in and keep your feet warm by the oil stove." She led Rene into her tiny living room, and the two of them plopped down on the small settee that was only about three feet from the stove, the warmth of which Rene welcomed. Pearl grabbed Rene's hand and held onto it as if Rene might disappear at any moment.

"The men who work for the Guard on the Great Lakes usually get relocated to a different station on the Lakes," Pearl said. "But the Southwest Harbor station is on an island in the Atlantic Ocean. Salt water!" And she cried some more. "What are we going to do?"

"You and Richard are going to welcome the opportunity," Rene said, matter-of-factly.

"But…"

Rene shushed her friend. "No buts. Let's look at this in a positive light. You and Richard are in love. It doesn't matter where you are as long as you have each other."

"But it's…"

"Ah, ah, ah!" Rene put her hand up like a policeman at a crosswalk. "Just wait. Hear me out."

Pearl hung her head and said, barely audible, "Okay."

"Now, I know you had big plans for your wedding."

Pearl nodded, her head down.

"And I know you've already hired Liliana to make your dress. But has she actually started on it?"

"Don't know," Pearl said, her head still hanging.

Rene rubbed her chin. "We need to find out how soon she can have it finished. If it's the one you showed me in the pattern book, it's probably not terribly involved for someone as practiced as Liliana."

Pearl looked up. "It is pretty simple, but she was counting on having another couple of months to work on it. I have no idea how many other projects she has going, how many other things are already promised to people before mine."

"How long before you leave?" Rene asked.

"Richard goes next week to find a place for us to live on the island, then he'll come back here and do a one-week orientation for the new guy who's taking over, and then we'll go. For good. I'll never see you again. And we'll be on the ocean. I'll have to learn about tides and cooking oysters and lobsters and…" She was sobbing, her head hanging down and tears falling onto her lap.

"Pearl, Pearl," Rene soothed her. "Think about the opportunities you'll have that you never would have had by staying here in Grand Marais. Or even somewhere else on the Great Lakes, for that matter."

"I don't want to think about that," Pearl said. She was now pouting like a belligerent toddler.

Rene reached over and put her hand under Pearl's chin, raising it so Pearl was forced to look up at her. "We can work this out. It's not the end of the world."

"Well, I feel like that's where I'm being forced to move to," Pearl said.

"What?"

"The end of the world. I feel like I'm going to be living at the end of the world."

Rene couldn't help but laugh, and she saw the corners of Pearl's mouth turn up. "When did Richard tell you about this?"

"Last night. I was in shock, and I didn't even cry until after he left. I kept telling myself I'd figure this all out. But the more I talked to myself about it, the more upset I became. I knew you'd be able to straighten me out. I can't allow him to see me like this. I'm a basket case. I need for him to think I'm okay with it. Please tell me you can do that…straighten me out, I mean." The look on her face was so pathetic, Rene began to doubt her own ability to bring Pearl around to thinking this was a good thing and *not* the end of the world.

"Okay, let's put this all into perspective," Rene said, settling back into a comfortable position. She knew she'd be there a while.

They discussed the issue for more than two hours. In the end, they decided to ask Liliana if she could possibly have the dress finished sooner so the wedding could still take place there in Grand Marais. If so, Pearl and Richard could still be married at the Lutheran church when he came back from finding a residence in the little town of Southwest Harbor.

Pearl had learned from Richard that the Southwest Harbor Station had only been opened in 1937, so it was nearly new, and he was both thrilled and honored to be asked to take over a place of such renown. Of course, he had a lot to learn about working on the ocean as opposed to Lake Superior, but he was excited, and that made it a little easier for Pearl to accept, once Rene convinced her how special it would be for Richard.

"I've been horribly selfish about this," Pearl admitted to Rene when they walked to the door.

"Don't think of it like that," Rene said. "You were totally overwhelmed by the whole thing and hadn't had enough time to think it through. It's as if a huge wall was erected overnight, right in front of you. You couldn't see around it or over it or through it, so you were overpowered by the magnitude of it. You couldn't imagine the good in it. Now you can, and you understand how important it is to make the best of this for the sake of Richard's and your happiness."

"You always know what to say to get me to the finish line without losing the race in the first few steps," Pearl said. "This isn't about me or Richard; it's about both of us…together. I know I'm going to miss you and Alvie and Ruby and Opal and Grand Marais and Lake Superior. But I need to step back and see it through Richard's eyes, as well. After all, he, too is leaving the place he loves."

"You're absolutely right. If you want to lead the orchestra, you have to turn your back on the crowd."[22]

Richard left for Maine on March tenth and returned on the twentieth. He borrowed a camera from one of the other Coasties at the station on the island and took pictures of everything there: the station, the town, the ferry, the house where he and Pearl would be living. He was obviously excited to show the photos to everyone, and everyone was excited to see them.

Liliana had no trouble getting the dress finished in time for the wedding on March twenty-sixth. Without Pearl knowing about it, Rene had paid Liliana some extra money to get the dress done in time. It was a small ceremony, but Rene could tell that Pearl was elated to have gotten married in her hometown, at her own church, with her remaining family and her friends around her. Ruby and Opal were both there, and a picture of Garnet sat on the table with the cake and the other refreshments.

After the ceremony, Pearl and Rene were standing by the refreshment table eating cake and reminiscing. Looking at Garnet's photo, Pearl said, "I know she wasn't the most pleasant person to be around. But at least she got to be here for a happy moment, even if it was only in spirit."

For the first time, Rene understood that a family can love even its most difficult member; that they can be not only understanding but also forgiving. And, to her surprise, she was finally able to erase her ill feelings about Garnet and Emmo's relationship, though she couldn't help but recognize that a large portion of her forgiveness was due to the passage of time and her remarkable interconnection with Alvie.

On the sunny morning when Pearl and Richard Houghton's car disappeared beyond the bend in the road, Rene could not speak, and she could barely breathe knowing that both she and Pearl would try to find new ways to fill the void that now, through no fault of their own, prevailed in their long-term friendship. She was sadly aware that her treasured relationship with her longest existing and dearest female friend would most likely wane at the hand of fate. She had to face the fact that, from here on out, it was likely that a relationship which had once been so personal would now struggle to survive through only occasional long-distance telephone calls, dwindling letters, and eventually just a yearly Christmas card containing a short handwritten note.

In January of 1944, the 1ˢᵗ Ukranian Front of the Red Army entered Poland. The first Victory Ship was launched. The RAF dropped 2,300 tons of bombs on Berlin. When February rolled around, Leipzig, Germany, was bombed for two consecutive nights. In March, heavy bombing occurred in Vienna, Austria. Three-hundred thirty-five Italians were killed (including seventy-five Jews) in a German response to a bomb blast that had killed German troops.

In the midst of all that, Rene cried repeatedly, not only because of the war, but also for herself. She had lost the comfort of thinking Pearl would always be there for her, and though she was aware that her sadness was selfish and only miniscule when compared to the problems of the rest of the world, she still felt sorry for herself. Alvie was doing his best to console her, but even his loving concern was not enough to alleviate her heavyheartedness; he told her only time would ease her pain.

In April, the Japanese launched "Operation Ichi-Go"[23] in central China where American bombers were located. In Devon, England, hundreds of American soldiers and sailors were killed over a two-day period in a training exercise in preparation for "Operation Overlord."

But more sadness found its way into Rene's already depressed mood.

In early May, the first transportation of Hungarian Jews to Auschwitz began—up to 14,000 per day. A failed attempt to assassinate Hitler occurred on July 20. On July 23, the advancing Soviet Red Army liberated the first death camp (Majdanek), but the next day, Greek Jews in Rhodes were deported to Auschwitz.

June was a decisive month for the war on several fronts: 1) five thousand bombs were dropped on German gun batteries on the Normandy coast in preparation for D-Day, 2) 155,000 Allied troops in Normandy pushed through the Atlantic Wall, the largest amphibious military operation in history, and 3) in a town near Limoges, France, 642 men, women, and children were killed in a German response to resistance activities. The United States Fifth Fleet won a decisive naval battle over the Imperial Japanese Navy; more than 200 Japanese planes were shot down, and the Americans lost only 29. In "Operation Bagration" (enacted to clear German forces from Belarus), the Soviets destroyed the German Army Group Center; this was considered the greatest defeat of the Wehrmacht during the entire war.

By early July, the Japanese had lost over 30,000 troops, and numerous civilians committed suicide at the encouragement of the Japanese military. An elaborately staged Nazi propaganda ruse early in the month of July, which was designed to portray the extermination camps as benign, was recognized as such by the Red Cross, but Miklós Horthy, Regent of the Kingdom of Hungary, halted the transportations of Hungarian Jews. FDR announced he would run for a fourth term as President of the United States. The Japanese military forces continued to be defeated. An assassination attempt was made on Hitler by Col. Claus von Stauffenberg, but it failed. Majdanak Concentration Camp was the first of many to be liberated by the Soviet forces.

On August 1, the Warsaw Uprising began. Four days later, 40,000-50,000 civilians were murdered by German and collaborating Russian forces in the Wola District of Warsaw. The next day, Germans rounded up young men in Krakow to thwart a potential uprising there. On August 21, the Dumbarton Oaks Conference began to set up the basic structure of the United Nations.
In September, Nazi authorities fled the Drancy concentration camp,

and it was taken by the French Red Cross. The final transportation of Dutch Jews from Westerbork left for Auschwitz. American troops reached the west wall of Germany's defense system. The Germans surrendered at Boulogne.

On October 7, Crematorium IV at Auschwitz was destroyed in the Sonderkommando Uprising. Miklós Horthy's government in Hungary was overthrown on October 15, and the deportations to Auschwitz were resumed under the Government of National Unity. October 21 marked the occupation of Aachen, the first German city to be captured.

November 5 marked Adolf Eichmann's authorization of the first death marches to the Budapest Ghetto. FDR was elected to an unrepeated fourth term as U.S. president. On November 20, Hitler left his headquarters at Rastenberg, East Prussia, never to return; he went to Berlin and would soon establish himself in the bunker there. On November 25, Heinrich Himmler ordered the gas chambers of Auschwitz destroyed as incriminating evidence of genocide.

On December 16, the Battle of the Bulge began.

A REVELATION

It was three nights before Christmas Eve. Rene and Alvie were sitting in the chairs that faced the fireplace, only the glow of the fire lighting the room. They were leisurely sipping eggnog, and the radio was on, the volume low, uninterrupted Christmas music being broadcast over the station. Rene was completely relaxed, and her eyelids were heavy. Without warning, the carol that had been quietly playing stopped abruptly, and news of the war blared out at her and Alvie.

"Is it any wonder my moods are so erratic?" Rene said to Alvie. Her eyes filled with tears. "This should be a joyous time, and yet here we are listening to someone talk about the horror going on around the world. I can't begin to imagine how you must have felt—over and over again—when you were guiding all the poor, lost souls whose families were not only hearing about it, as we are, but actually experiencing it." Thoughts about Liliana crossed her mind, and her mood soured ten-fold in a matter of only a second.

"Bear in mind that I'm here for you," Alvie told her, his voice calm and soothing. "Just because I'm no longer a guide, it doesn't mean I'm not still here for you, Irene. Oolanaloo wants you to find peace. And so do I."

"In the midst of all this?" Rene asked derisively, angrily gesturing toward the radio. "How strong does he think I am?"

"He knows you're much stronger than *you* think you are," Alvie said. "I know this as a fact as well."

"I can't do it. I can't take it anymore." Her fists were clenched, and her breathing was irregular; she was on the verge of tears.

"Perhaps not at this moment," Alvie consoled her, "but you *will* find more strength buried deep inside yourself. I've seen you uncover it before, and I know you're capable of finding it again. Oolanaloo knows it too."

"You're wrong," Rene snapped. "Both of you." Her face was red with anger.

Alvie slowly rose and walked calmly to her. He stopped in front of her, his face wracked with pain. "May I hold you?" he asked quietly.

Rene sat there momentarily, looking up at him, her pain and anger causing her to doubt that even Alvie's comforting embrace could make her feel better. Then, without warning, something stirred inside her head. She wasn't certain if it was a voice or merely something she felt; she couldn't positively identify it. The experience was completely foreign to her, and it slowly crept over her entire body.

She could see Alvie spreading his arms, inviting her into the warmth of his protective embrace, and she was somehow assured that the act really would alleviate her wrought-up emotions. But while she anticipated rising and succumbing to his invitation, a strange thing happened: without any effort on her part, her body floated and melted into the cradle of Alvie's arms. Everything around her became ethereal, and she transcended into a hypnogogic state. She was not controlling her movements; she was neither encouraging them nor fighting them. She was merely allowing herself to be manipulated by something over which she had no control, and she had no intention of subduing it.

She was still sitting in the chair when she realized Alvie was speaking to her. "Tell me about it," he said.

Slowly, she looked up at Alvie. She blinked. "I…I…heard… no, I think I *saw* what Oolanaloo was saying. Oolanaloo spoke to me, but I didn't hear anything. I didn't really see anything, either. It was just… just…there."

He took her hand and knelt in front of her. "What do you remember feeling?" he asked.

"Softness. Yes. It was soft. And tender. And gentle. And entirely comprehendible."

Alvie's face shone as if a bright light had been directed at him.

Rene looked away. Her brows came together suggesting a complete lack of understanding, though her brain was obviously trying to process everything that had just happened. Eventually her face brightened, and she smiled and closed her eyes, sighing peacefully. Then she looked at Alvie. She was glowing, and she said, "I know Oolanaloo now."

Alvie was ecstatic. He jumped up and spun around. "I *knew* you had communicated with Oolanaloo. And it was on a level beyond anything you have ever dreamed of, wasn't it?"

"Was it actually physical?" Rene asked.

"It was *total*. Did it feel physical to you?"

She started to speak, but she stopped, wanting to make sure she could describe it exactly as she had experienced it. Alvie waited patiently. Then Rene said, "I'm having trouble putting it into words. I didn't just *hear* Oolanaloo; I *felt* every word. I was somewhere else, yet I don't remember moving." She put her hand on her forehead. "How can that be?"

"It was what Oolanaloo calls a 'celestial merge.' It was virtual; your mind caused your body to experience every suggestion your brain made, yet you were not actually participating physically."

"It was the most exhilarating thing I've ever…I can't even explain how it…how I…"

Alvie sat down on the floor at her feet and leaned against the chair, resting his head on her thigh.

Rene was exhausted. She closed her eyes and sighed, a small moaning sound escaping her lips, the hint of a contented smile evident on her face.

HELLO 1945

On New Year's Eve, Alvie and Rene joined the Gustavsons and Liliana to celebrate the passing of one year and the ushering in of the next. Polly had come home from Petoskey for the holidays. Rene enjoyed listening to her talk about her life away from what she called "the confines of Grand Marais."

At one point during the evening, Malcolm looked at his daughter and Liliana, both talking at the same time, and said, "I don't think the two of them have stopped jabbering since Polly got here."

"They obviously have a lot to catch up on," Rene said. She was feeling the sting of having lost the one female friend she could always count on when she needed to talk.

"You must miss Pearl terribly," Beatrice said.

Rene hung her head, embarrassed, and asked, "Is it that obvious?"

"Yes, and it should be," Beatrice answered. "Friendships—*true* friendships—are hard to come by."

At just a few minutes before midnight, they all donned their winter apparel and stepped out onto the Gustavsons' porch. The night was clear, there was no wind, and the stars were twinkling. Malcolm turned the radio up so they could hear it outside, and they all welcomed in the new year, along with whoops and shouts and even some firecrackers from various residences around town. Rene and Alvie kissed, and Malcolm and Beatrice followed suit. They all hugged each other, wishing everyone a "happier" new year.

Rene and Alvie silently walked arm-in-arm to her house. She hated knowing that he would say goodnight to her then depart to the building behind the church where he lived. But that was the arrangement they had to follow. When they reached her front stoop, Alvie said, "Don't you think it's time we began living together?"

Rene looked at him, desperately wanting to agree but knowing it would be frowned upon by the whole town. Her smile faded, and she hung her head. "Oh, Alvie, we've been through this a hundred times."

"Then let's make it official. Marry me."

1945 – January through June

"You're having trouble wrapping your head around the idea, aren't you?" Alvie asked Rene.

"I'm doing what with my head?"

"You're having trouble accepting the idea of us getting married, right?"

Rene sighed. "Come inside. It's too cold to stand out here and discuss this." They went in. Rene took off her coat; Alvie left his on. "Aren't you going to stay a while so we can talk about this?" she asked him.

Alvie didn't budge, he just looked at her, a blank expression on his face.

"Alvie, please. We need to discuss some really important issues. I *do* want to marry you, probably more than anything else I've ever done. But we don't share a normal life."

Alvie threw his hands into the air. "Oh, for crying out loud, Irene. What in the name of Oolanaloo is 'a normal life'? We've known each other for years now, and I don't mean in an 'acquaintance' sort of way; I mean we really *know* each other. Can you deny that?"

"No, of course I can't." She was on the verge of anger. "But we only have a few short years left to spend together, and I don't want to stand in the way of you doing what comes naturally to you. You'll still be here when I die, and you'll be sticking around forever after I'm gone. I don't understand enough about the way you've lived for eons, or the way you interpret what's going on right now in our lives. That thought, for me, isn't as simple as taking a dose of medicine and hoping all the symptoms just go away. It's all too much for me to…what did you call it? Wrap my head around? I'm mortal; you're not."

"Irene, I understand your…"

"No!" she snapped at him. "Let me finish. You straightened me out after everything that happened to me, from my parents to my husband and my child, to say nothing about what's going on all over the world right now. In addition, without any suggestion on my part, you introduced me to more things, more situations, than any human is capable of imagining, let alone accomplishing. You've given me opportunities beyond my wildest dreams. But I can't live knowing you'll bear the pain of human loss when I can no longer be with you. Don't get me wrong; I'm not putting myself up on a pedestal, here. I'm not trying to say you'll whine and cry and grieve forever, but I *am* being a realist. I know how humans think. I know that living every day and being aware that you and I are bonded in a way I could never have imagined, and then thinking about how you'll feel when I have to leave you behind, presents me with a kind of pain I can't bear. You might as well reach inside my chest and yank the heart right out of me."

She whirled away from him, wrapping her arms around herself. "If we get any closer—and marriage *will* make us closer—I'll go crazy thinking about the final days we'll spend together." She turned back to him and softened her voice. "I cherish every moment I'm with you, Alvie Wybel, and I think you feel the same. But if things were reversed—if you were mortal and I were immortal—the idea of knowing I'd be devastated when I no longer had you with me would be something *you'd* have a hard time facing, wouldn't it?"

Alvie closed his eyes. "Please stop," he whispered. His trembling hands covered his face. "How could I have been so blind?" He looked up at the ceiling. "I don't understand. I can still read your thoughts, yet somehow I've allowed myself to overlook them, to let this happen without realizing the torture it was causing you. Why couldn't I see it?" He dropped his hands and hung his head. "Forgive me, Irene. I had no intentions of…"

Rene threw herself at Alvie, wrapping her arms around him,

and he locked his arms around her. He put his forehead against hers, sighed a befuddled sigh, and said, "I've been waiting for the right moment to tell you, Irene. But in delaying, I've made you miserable, the exact opposite of what I intended. Oolanaloo was right; I should have told you immediately, but my new humanness created an unforeseen problem; it caused you to misinterpret my intentions. Oh, I'm so sorry. *So, so* sorry."

"Tell me what?" Rene asked, her voice more apologetic than accusatory. She could feel his heartbeat increase and hear his breathing become rapid and shallow. She backed away from him. Questioning lines ran deeply through her face, and her eyes begged him for an explanation.

He removed his coat. Then he took her by the hand and led her to the kitchen table where he proceeded to pull out a chair for her; she sat. He filled the teakettle with water, lit the stove, and put the kettle on to heat, all the while remaining silent. Rene did not interrupt, she merely sat and watched. Alvie removed two cups and saucers from the hutch, took down the sugar bowl, and put them all on the table. Then he removed the pitcher of cream from the refrigerator and grabbed two spoons out of the drawer beside the sink; he put them on the table beside the sugar bowl. He removed two tea bags from the tea canister and placed one in each of the cups. He walked to the stove, keeping his back toward Rene while he silently waited for the water to boil.

When the kettle started to whistle, Alvie turned off the heat, removed the kettle from the burner, and walked to the table where he poured both cups full. He put the kettle back on the stove, then he sat down opposite Rene, picked up a spoon, and began stirring. Rene watched the water in his cup change to a light brown-orange color. Finally, he looked up at Rene, and their eyes met.

Alvie swallowed. In a low voice he said, "For the first time, I have begun to understand what it is to be human. I have always thought I knew, but it took *becoming* human to begin to understand the complexity of it. I've never given you—meaning all humans—enough credit for your accomplishments. Even though I was responsible for helping you through your most difficult times, I never fully understood what you were dealing with. And yet Oolanaloo let me continue. No, *urged* me to continue." He shook his head. "Why would Oolanaloo do that?"

Rene said, very matter-of-factly, "Oolanaloo knew you were capable of handling it. You certainly proved yourself over time. Think of the number of humans whose deepest woes you've alleviated because of your understanding."

"But I see now that what I thought was complete understanding was just my egotistical attitude rather than true empathy. I thought I was the high and mighty intermediary between Oolanaloo and every human. I thought I could put an end to every human's suffering. But now I realize, *I* needed help, too."

"So Oolanaloo sent you to someone who could rattle you," Rene said. "I remember you saying to me once that you weren't sure if you were the one doing the guiding or vice versa."

Alvie closed his eyes. "I do remember saying that. I was just being flippant; I didn't consider that it might actually be true when I said it."

"There is not one human alive who doesn't suffer to some degree; it's just a part of us, I guess," Rene said. "But you haven't dealt only with humans. You've been responsible for the elevation of spirit in beings we humans can't even picture in our heads. Don't belittle yourself because you reached a snag in one human relationship. And don't, for one instant, think our relationship is like any other you've ever had. I know you well enough to know you wouldn't be in the mental state you're in right now if you had experienced this before."

Alvie looked at her, and Rene could read the confusion on his face. He spoke softly, "I don't know how you do it. You have, with only a few words, made me aware of the depth of the human psyche, something that, until this very minute, I had dismissed as an impossibility in humans." His face turned red, and he looked away from her. "Please don't take offense at that remark. How could I have been so wrong? How could Oolanaloo let me go on thinking that?"

"Perhaps because Oolanaloo knew you needed to *become* human so you could better understand not only human weakness and ignorance, but also our resourcefulness and comprehension. Believe it or not, some of us do have an unprecedented amount of foresight."

"Why would Oolanaloo know that and not teach me?" Alvie asked.

"Because not all learning is the result of being taught. As humans, we learn more by experience than by any other means. But you already know that, so don't take it personally, Alvie. If there are as many guides as you say there are, I'm sure Oolanaloo had every intention of eventually getting around to making sure you would become aware of it. But reaching every guide must take time, and there hasn't been a whole lot of time in the history of humankind. You said yourself that our earth is only an infant in this *one* universe and that human inhabitants have been around for no more than a blink of the eye in terms of the total existence of time. And I have no reason to doubt that fact; you've never lied to me."

Alvie was looking at her like she was a stranger. He mechanically raised his cup, took a sip of his tea, and then looked past her, into the distance. Rene saw his face slowly change. The worry lines softened and began to dissipate. He didn't blink; his gaze was fixed on a spot just over her head. His mouth went from being turned down at the corners to showing a hint of a smile. She fought the urge to turn and see if someone—or something—was there. Then Alvie lowered his gaze, looked her in the eyes, and said, "Oolanaloo will speak to you now."

Rene was eager to feel Oolanaloo speak. She closed her eyes and cleared her thoughts. Just as when Alvie had taken her to Birkenau, she was aware of instantly being in unfamiliar surroundings. But these surroundings were inviting, comforting. She waited for Oolanaloo's voice, but there was no sound. She was, instead, enveloped by a calming, entirely pleasant presence. There were aromas she had not experienced before, or at least had not been aware of.

She was only wrapped up in the presence for a matter of seconds, but the message was clear, and she was jolted back to her own kitchen with Alvie sitting across from her, sipping his tea. She took a deep breath and smiled at him. "You're right. You should have told me as soon as you knew."

A NEW WORLD OPENS UP

In a private ceremony in Marquette, the Justice of the Peace (his wife and daughter acting as witnesses) married Rene and Alvie during a late January thaw. They exchanged rings, a custom that had recently become popular in the United States. Until the middle of the twentieth century, it was customary for only the wife to wear a wedding ring. But both Rene and Alvie liked the idea of having a little token of love and devotedness they could carry with them.

Alvie moved into Rene's house, just as she had hoped he'd do. She had been afraid he might want to find a different place for the two of them to live, but she didn't want to move to another house; the fact that this house had been built on the same property where she'd grown up made it extremely special to her. She was pleased to learn that Alvie felt the same way about it. He decided to pass his church-cleaning job to a young man who desperately needed some money (even though the wage was meager, to say the least).

"There's something I've never asked you, Alvie," Rene said to him on their way home from Marquette.

"Fire away," Alvie said.

"Okay," Rene answered, a questioning look crossing her face. She was not completely sure he had meant he wanted her to ask, but she assumed that was his meaning, so she continued. "I know you didn't earn much working at the church, so where have you been getting enough money to live on and to buy our rings? I tried not to interfere in something I figured was none of my business, but I remember you turning me down a couple of times when I offered to pay for something."

"Oolanaloo always took care of that," he said, as if it should be no surprise.

"How?"

"I never needed money until I began guiding humans," he said. "Other places don't trade currency for items—they either barter or simply give things to others who need them. But when I began guiding humans, I had to carry a pouch of some sort for when it was mandatory that I 'buy' something, which wasn't very often because I usually didn't stay in any one place for very long. I didn't eat, so I didn't have to buy food, and I took care of designing my own clothing." He looked at Rene and grinned sheepishly. "Whenever I needed money, I only had to pull out my pouch, and there was the necessary currency, compliments of Oolanaloo."

"And that was the set-up here, too? When you were working at the church, I mean."

"Well, I'll admit it's been a bit more difficult, but whatever the church gave me, Oolanaloo duplicated it. I didn't really have much to spend it on."

"So you were able to save enough for our wedding trip and the rings?"

"Huh…I never consciously thought about saving money, but yes, I guess I did save some."

"You seriously have never had any concerns about money?"

He shrugged. "None. And Oolanaloo has assured me we will continue to receive money in the same way."

"Holy whah!"

In mid-January Red Army troops entered Warsaw, and the Allied Forces officially won the Battle of the Bulge. On January 27, the Soviets entered the concentration camp at Auschwitz. On January 31, the Red Army crossed the Oder River into Germany, which put them less than fifty miles from Berlin. FDR, Churchill, and Stalin met in Yalta on February 2 to plan the end of WWII in both theaters and to discuss the ramifications of the Soviets, who controlled most of Eastern Europe.

Rene had forgotten how satisfying it was to be married. "Marriage agrees with me," she told Alvie one day.

He gave her that smile she so loved and said, "And I never imagined it could *be so* pleasurable, so engaging, so amusing. So *awesome*! And we have the rest of eternity to enjoy it."

"Now that I've had time to think about it, I'm really kind of glad you waited for Oolanaloo to tell me that I'm going to be with you forever. I never imagined *my* immortality was in the plan."

Alvie frowned, and his sudden mood change was obvious to Rene. He said, dejectedly, "Oolanaloo urged me to tell you about the immortality, but I didn't want to spring it on you immediately; I wanted to wait for exactly the right moment." He looked away from her. "I know, now, that was not the smartest thing I could have done."

"Water under the bridge," Rene said. "Though I must admit, I'm having a bit of trouble…um…wrapping my head around the whole thing." She grinned at Alvie. "Did I use that correctly?"

"You're a quick study," he said, grinning back.

On February 3, the Battle of Manilla began when U.S. and Philippine forces attacked the Japanese, and the "Manilla Massacre"[24] took place during the fighting. There was heavy bombing of Berlin. On February 19, the U.S. Marines invaded Iwo Jima and raised the American flag on Mount Suribachi after four days of fighting. On February 25, the U.S. made a B-29 incendiary raid on Tokyo.

The Battle of Remagen occurred on March 7 when the U.S. First Army captured the Ludendorff Bridge over the Rhine River and began crossing into Germany. On March 10, Japanese Fu-Go balloon bombs damaged the Manhattan Project site in Washington state with no lasting effects. The next day, hundreds of B-29s firebombed Nagoya, Japan. On March 19, sixty Jews were killed during the "Deutsch Schutzen Massacre." Tokyo continued to be bombed, and General Patton's troops captured Mainz, Germany. March 22-23 saw the crossing of the Rhine by British and U.S. forces at Oppenheim, making it obvious that Germany was under attack from all sides. On March 29, the Red Army entered Austria, and the Germans were in retreat all over the center of the country. The next day, Red Army forces captured Danzig, and on March 31, General Eisenhower broadcasted a demand for the German surrender.

Early April brought the liberation of the Ohrdruf death camp by the

Allies, and Buchenwald concentration camp was liberated by American forces.

LILIANA'S TURNING POINT

By mid-April of 1945, most of the snow had melted in and around Grand Marais. It had been an extremely warm winter with only minimal snowfall. Liliana had been saving up money to buy a car of her own, even though it was unusual for women to do a lot of driving. Beatrice and Malcolm told her she could use their vehicle whenever she wanted, but she was dead set on buying one so she could go to visit Polly whenever she felt the urge and not leave the Gustavsons without a vehicle for an extended period of time. Up to that point, every time she had made the trip, Malcolm had driven her to the ferry dock in St. Ignace, and Polly had picked her up in Mackinac City.

"I will drive to Polly's house whenever I want to see her if I have my own car," she told Beatrice and Malcolm. "I will not need you to be taxicab. I will find car in Petoskey better than here in U.P. More options there," she said. So Malcolm drove her to St. Ignace and watched her board the ferry. Liliana was all smiles as she waved good-bye to him, knowing she would return to Grand Marais in her own car.

A week later, Liliana drove up to the Gustavsons' home in a used 1942 Nash. She and Polly had done a lot of looking in Petoskey, and when they came across that particular car, Liliana said, "This car is it." She had learned that, at the beginning of 1942, new car sales had been suspended because of a rationing program. Congress issued a declaration that new automobiles would no longer be built with any chrome (with the exception of the bumpers). Chrome came from Rhodesia, but the ships that normally delivered the chromed parts to the U.S. were needed to move troops and supplies to Britain. So parts that were normally chromed would, instead, be painted black. Those vehicles quickly earned the name "blackout trim" models, and on February 3 of 1942, the final Nash rolled off the line with its chromeless "blackout trim." There would be no more new Nash cars manufactured until peace was declared.

The salesman at the dealership where Liliana and Polly found the car promised it would deliver 25 to 30 miles per each gallon of gasoline. He showed them an old advertisement he'd found in the glove box: "...the big Nash still scampers through traffic like an All-American half-back... Rides the curves like a locomotive... Streaks over winter ruts as serenely as a gull clipping the waves." Of course, having lived on the shores of Lake Superior, the words appealed to Liliana since she could identify with the gulls "clipping the waves."

When she arrived in Grand Marais in her new car, Malcolm, Beatrice, Rene, and Alvie were all there to meet her. They ooh'd and aah'd over it, and Alvie even took it for a spin. He had discovered that he *loved* driving and couldn't get enough of it. He gave Liliana his approval, and she grinned from ear to ear. "I will go back to Polly's house in June. It will take more money to cross on ferry with car, but it will mean no one have to meet me on this side or other," she said, proudly.

Later that afternoon, she announced to everyone, "I will become American citizen soon. I study and get better at speaking. Also, I know United States history." She had been reading a lot of American books, especially history books, and as a result, her vocabulary and speech patterns were becoming more and more English and less and less Polish. She sidled up to Malcolm and poked him in the arm. "Ask me question, Mister Papa."

"All right. Who was the first President of the United States?"

Liliana waved her hand in the air. "Too easy—George Washington. Ask me harder one."

Malcolm thought for a moment. "What are the three branches of the United States government?"

She answered without hesitation. "Legislative, Executive, Judicial."

"But now, here's the hard part...what does each branch do?"

"Not so hard," Liliana said, a smug smile crossing her lips. "Legislative branch make laws. Executive enforce laws. Judicial interpret laws."

"When was the American Civil War?" Beatrice asked.

"1861 to 1865. I am now reading American Civil War book, so I can talk all about it. Honest Abe Lincoln was president during war. North and South fought because of slavery. North wanted to ablo…abo…"

"Abolish it," Alvie said.

"Yes, thank you. North won, but slaves had hard times ahead becoming recognized as free citizens." She pursed her lips. "Not only hard for Negroes after American Civil War. Also for people in countries all over world after wars. Even right up to now," she said, sadness in her voice.

Everyone looked silently at Liliana. She brightened up, smiled, and said, "Not bad for Polish woman, huh?"

"Excellent for Polish woman!" Rene said. "I'm not sure I could have answered all those questions so quickly."

On April 20, Hitler celebrated his 56th birthday in the bunker in Berlin, but he was reported to have been in failing health, being "nervous and depressed." On April 23, Hitler stripped Hermann Göring of all his offices and expelled him from the Nazi Party. On April 27, the encirclement of the German forces in Berlin was completed. Heinrich Himmler, ignoring Hitler's orders, made a secret surrender offer to the Allies, but Hitler heard of the betrayal on April 28 and ordered Himmler shot. Mussolini, though heavily disguised, was captured while trying to escape to Switzerland. He and his mistress were shot and hanged upside down by the feet in Milan. On April 29, Dachau concentration camp was liberated by the U.S. Army. On the same date, Hitler married Eva Braun, but the next day, they committed suicide. Joseph Goebbels was appointed Reich Chancellor and Grand Admiral Karl Dönitz was appointed Reich President.

On May 1, Goebbels and his wife murdered their children and committed suicide. On May 2, the Battle of Berlin ended when the commander, who was no longer bound by Goebbels' commands, surrendered the city of Berlin, unconditionally, to the Soviets. On the fourth of May, Karl Dönitz ordered all U-boats to cease operations, and the Neuengamme concentration camp was liberated that same day. On May 5, Mauthausen concentration camp was liberated, and Japanese fire balloons claimed lives at a Sunday school group in Bly,

Oregon. On May 7, Germany surrendered unconditionally to the Allies at the Western Allied Headquarters in France. Herman Göring, in the hands of the SS, surrendered to the Americans. May 8 became Victory in Europe Day (VE Day). On May 21, Heinrich Himmler, Commander of the SS, was arrested by Soviet troops. He attempted to pass himself off as a common soldier, but he ended up being handed over to a British interrogation center on May 23, and he committed suicide by swallowing a cyanide pill.

In early June, Liliana took her citizenship test and became a U.S. citizen. On June 15, she left Grand Marais to visit Polly. She bubbled over with obvious excitement as she loaded her suitcase into the Nash, said goodbye to her adopted family, and set out for Petoskey for the first time by herself.

At 10:30 PM that night, the Gustavsons received a call from Polly: Liliana had not arrived. Early the next morning, Beatrice knocked on Rene and Alvie's door.

"You're up bright and early," Rene said as she rubbed the sleep from her eyes.

"Sorry to bother you so early. Liliana is missing."

The statement hit Rene like a bolt out of the blue. "What?"

Beatrice continued, "She was to meet Polly at lunchtime yesterday. When she hadn't shown up by mid-afternoon, Polly called the St. Ignace, Mackinac City, and Petoskey Police Departments to report her missing. They told her they could check with a couple of other nearby police departments to see if there had been an accident reported, but there was nothing else they could do until she had been missing for twenty-four hours," she said, incredulity evident in her voice.

"Come in, Beatrice," Rene said. "Alvie should hear this, too."

He had risen before Rene and was in the bathroom shaving. Rene tapped on the door. "Yes, my love?" he opened the door and greeted her with a face covered in shaving soap lather.

"Liliana's missing."

"Oh, no," Alvie said. He grabbed a towel and wiped his face.

"Beatrice is here. Come out, and let's get the whole story."

Alvie put on pants and a shirt and came hurrying out, barefooted, hair askew, and still buttoning his shirt. "What's this about?"

"Liliana was supposed to be at Polly's workplace for lunch yesterday, but she never showed up," Beatrice said. Her voice was unwavering…rock solid.

How can she remain so calm at a time like this? Rene wondered.

Alvie looked at Rene and said, "Yes, how?" He turned back to Beatrice and asked, "Did Polly call the police?"

"St. Ignace, Mackinac City, and Petoskey. They said there's nothing they can do until she's been missing for twenty-four hours."

"Do you want us to help you look for her?" Rene asked. "I mean, if she had an accident along the way, the car might go unnoticed; there are some pretty mean drop-offs along Lake Michigan on US-2."

Beatrice inhaled a couple of hiccupped breaths, the only indication that she was worried. "I'm not sure if she went down 77 or 117. She could have had trouble before she even reached US-2."

"Then we need to split up and check both routes. You and Malcolm go one way, Alvie and I will go the other. We can meet up in St. Ignace. By that time, it will have been close to the 24-hour mark because she'll have been missing since lunchtime yesterday. In the meantime, can Polly take time off work to look for her along the usual route they take from the ferry to her workplace?"

"We discussed that, and Polly wants to stay there in case Liliana calls or shows up," Beatrice said. "Malcolm won't leave home in case either Liliana or Polly calls." Beatrice took a deep breath. "And there's something else." She lowered her head and absentmindedly rubbed her forehead. "Malcolm and I have both noticed that Liliana has been looking at a lot of maps lately. We just assumed it had something to do with studying for her citizenship test." She raised her head back up, put her hand on her chest, and looked at Rene. "But last night we went into her room and found that most of them were of the Eastern United States. I don't know what significance that has, but it just seemed odd to us." Her eyes welled up with tears, and she swallowed what must have been an enormous lump in her throat. She looked at Alvie. "Do you suppose she's been planning to go somewhere else?"

"It's a possibility," Alvie said. "Does she know anyone who lives on the east coast?"

"Not that I'm aware of," Beatrice said.

Rene had been silently running through the evidence Beatrice had given them. She had an idea, albeit a bad-tasting one.

Alvie jerked his head toward Rene, and he grabbed her by the arm. She looked up at him, knowing he was aware of her train of thought.

Beatrice, obviously noticing their strange behavior, asked, "Do you know something I should know?"

"It's only a thought," Rene said, "probably not worthy of consideration."

"I'm ready to jump at any chance of finding her," Beatrice said. She grabbed Rene by the other arm and asked, "What are you thinking?"

Rene gently pulled her arms back to her sides, and both Alvie and Beatrice let go of her. "It's just that, for the last few months, she's been distant, and when she does talk to me, she talks about Poland, Warsaw. About how much she misses it. About wanting to find where her parents were killed. She almost seemed obsessed with it. I hate to think she's been planning to go there without letting us know."

"Oh, Rene," Beatrice staggered, but Alvie caught her before she collapsed.

"It's just a possible theory, Beatrice," Rene said. "Probably not something we should even be concerned about. Silly me. Sometimes I let my mind wander, and my wild imagination takes over. I'm sorry. I didn't mean to scare you."

"I think you might be right," Beatrice said softly. "I've thought the same thing for a year. But every time I allowed myself to think it might be true, I'd do my best to convince myself that couldn't be possible." She looked back and forth between Rene and Alvie. "Could it?"

Both Alvie and Rene remained silent for a few seconds, and the realization that it could be possible was evident on Beatrice's face. It was, in fact, the only answer that made sense to Rene.

Beatrice straightened up to her full height, turned toward the door, and said, "I must get back home. I need to run this by Malcolm."

"We'll come with you," Alvie said. "You need all the support you can get right now, and so will Malcolm."

"Thank you," Beatrice said. "I'm sorry to expose you to our family problems, but…"

Alvie cut her off. "No apologies required. Or accepted. We're here for you. Don't ever think otherwise." He reached for his coat, but Rene reminded him that he should put on some socks and shoes before they left. Alvie blushed, raced to the bedroom where he grabbed a pair of socks, then came back to the entry bench and sat down, pulling them on, followed by his shoes. The three of them silently walked to the Gustavsons' house.

Following an intense conversation about the possibilities and the plans that should accompany them, they decided it would be best to leave the search up to the police. Malcolm spoke with the Petoskey Police Department who assured him they would do everything they could to find her. They took all the information they could glean from Beatrice, Malcolm, Rene, and Alvie, and they said they'd send someone over to Polly's workplace to get any information she might be able to add.

Polly was ninety-nine percent certain Liliana was on her way to the east coast where she could book passage on a ship to Europe, and she told the police about her idea. They organized a watch for her through cities along several routes that would lead Liliana to an east coast seaport. They knew the make and model and color of the car, the license number, and they each had a detailed description of Liliana. Though the prospect of actually finding her was slim, everyone kept their hopes high.

Two days passed without a word from either the police or

Liliana herself. On the third day, the Gustavsons received a letter that had been postmarked in St. Ignace; it was from Liliana. Evidently, she had mailed it before she boarded the ferry, hoping it would reach Malcolm and Beatrice within a few days. It explained her intent:

> *Najdroższy Beatrice i Mister Papa,*
>
> *I owe much grateful to you. Know, please, I love you as I would real parents. But I am not of your blood, and I must replenish my bond to real parents and real home near Warsaw. I will sail to Europe and then overland to reach Poland. I make promise to avoid Nazi-occupied countries; do not be scared for me. No one will know I am Jewish. I will appear as traveling in war effort to help sick and wounded. It will take many months, maybe year, but I will be fine. Please tell Polly.*
>
> *Liliana Bartosz*

What they did not know, nor suspect, is that Liliana crossed the Detroit River via the Ambassador Bridge from Detroit to Windsor, Ontario, Canada. She made her way to Toronto where she sold her car and boarded a cargo vessel. She proceeded to sail up the St. Lawrence Seaway to Montreal, where she was able to book passage on another ship carrying goods through the North Atlantic to Oslo, Norway. From there, she traveled by land, north through Sweden and back south through Finland, around the Baltic Sea. She then passed through the northwest corner of the Soviet Union and into Estonia, continuing through Latvia and Lithuania before reaching her beloved Poland, avoiding the Germans at all costs. She had "planted" the maps of the Eastern U.S. in her room at the Gustavsons' home to draw everyone off course in an effort to keep them from slowing or stopping her progress. No one, not even the police, would think she might attempt such an extensive journey.

1945 – July through December

THE EPIPHANY

Following a warmer-than-usual winter, the summer was countering by being unseasonably cool. On the late evening of Independence Day, people all over the U.P. donned winter coats, hats, and gloves to stand outside and watch the fireworks. Grand Marais was no exception. Even with the chill, the harbor was dotted with pleasure craft filled with bundled-up people waiting for the annual fireworks display, albeit somewhat shortened due to lack of funds and war-induced rationing. The fireworks were set off from the shore and aimed out over the harbor where, on a calm night, their bright colors would reflect beautifully in the water. But on July 4, 1945, a stiff breeze was blowing enough to keep the water's surface stirred up, so there were only broken reflections. On the plus side, however, the wind blew the smoke away quickly and allowed the spectators to see each of the explosions against the dark background of the sky without an airborne smokescreen hindering their view.

There had been no sign of Liliana—no reports from police, no letters, no calls—only lots of nothing. Beatrice and Malcolm were visibly depressed, but they kept themselves placated by reminding each other that no news was good news, meaning they could, at least, hope that she had not been caught, though Beatrice had mentioned to Rene several times that she longed for a letter or word of some kind.

"You know she can't send you something with a postmark on it because it would give her position away," Rene said. She and Beatrice had bumped into each other in the grocery store.

"I know it as well as anyone," Beatrice said. "But that doesn't keep me from wishing it."

"How's Polly taking it?" Rene asked. "You haven't mentioned her in a while."

"Pretty hard. She missed a week or more of work right after we got Liliana's only letter from St. Ignace. Said she just couldn't believe Liliana had set the whole thing up. She felt 'used' by Liliana."

"Oh, but she has to know…"

"Yes," Beatrice said, "she knows now that Liliana wasn't using her. It just took Polly some time to sort through the facts before she came to that conclusion. But at that point in time, Polly was heartsick and had to lay the blame somewhere. And she couldn't talk to anyone about it for fear of putting Liliana at risk of being discovered. That was the last thing she wanted to do, even though she felt betrayed. After Malcolm and I went to Petoskey and talked it all out with her, she understood that she was simply lashing out at Liliana because she knew she'd lost her best friend…lost for a long time, if not forever."

Rene's face drooped. "I know exactly how she felt."

Beatrice nodded.

The first test of a nuclear weapon was conducted on July 16 at Alamogordo, New Mexico. The Potsdam Conference began on July 17; Churchill, Stalin, and Truman agreed to insist upon the unconditional surrender of Japan. On July 26, Clement Attlee replaced Winston Churchill as Britain's Prime Minister (the Labour Party had won the general election by a landslide), and on that same date, the Potsdam Declaration (defining terms for Japanese surrender) was issued.

On August 6, the U.S. bomber Enola Gay *dropped the first atomic bomb ("Little Man") on Hiroshima, Japan. On August 9, the U.S. bomber* Bockscar *dropped a second atomic bomb ("Fat Boy") on Nagasaki, Japan. All U.S. combat units were frozen in place, and it went down in history as the last day of combat action. On August 15, Emperor Hirohito issued a radio broadcast announcing the surrender of Japan.*

The "Japanese Instrument of Surrender" was signed on September 2 on the deck of the USS Missouri *in Tokyo Bay, and the last German troops surrendered on the most remote and northerly of the main islands in Svalbard on September 4.*

    The end of the war with Japan, along with Germany's surrender, left the people of Grand Marais in high spirits. But the period from mid-September through early October was unusually windy for the U.P., and the leaves, which normally would have begun to change color, were sparse, as the majority of them were blown from the trees before getting a chance to display their autumn beauty. The sky was cloudy and gray on more days than it was clear and blue, and the result of that lack of sunlight was obvious in every person's attitude around town.

    Rene was no exception. "I don't know how much longer I can cope with all of the depression that's so evident around here," Rene said with a heavy sigh.

    Alvie, tilting his head to the side in an expression of sympathy, said, "I guess we just have to handle it as best we can since there's not much we can do to change it."

    "Oh, that really helped," Rene said, rolling her eyes. She was hoping he'd have some sort of magic that would erase it all and make it change. Alvie gave her an understanding look; she'd seen that look many times. But it didn't work any of the magic she was hoping for. "I wonder why God thinks this kind of depression is good for anyone," she said.

    Alvie's head snapped up, and his brow furrowed. Rene responded with raised eyebrows accompanying a *What kind of answer do you have to that?* expression.

    "You know my thoughts on your god perfectly well. There is no other than…"

    "I know. Oolanaloo."

    He sighed. "Irene, you have communicated directly with Oolanaloo in the past. Why do you refuse to accept that Oolanaloo is the only…?" His voice trailed off as he read her thoughts, and he seemed surprised by her apparent desire to discuss the topic.

    She stared directly into Alvie's eyes. She was wavering. "I

can't help but think there's a reason why Oolanaloo won't allow me to let go of my beliefs. I don't know if I'll ever find the real truth, or if there's even a real truth to find."

"I'm aware that you can't just let go of your beliefs overnight," Alvie said. "You have to completely understand Oolanaloo before you can do that and accept the truth. You have to trust Oolanaloo above all others, and that's a big step for a Christian human." He touched her cheek. "A man for whom I have the highest regard said, 'We dance 'round in a ring and suppose. The secret sits in the middle and knows.'[25]"

Rene admitted to herself that Alvie was right. She also knew she had never encountered a more pleasant experience than when hers and Oolanaloo's thoughts had entwined.

"Tell me something," Alvie said. "This is something I've never understood. When someone gets sick, for instance, you pray to your god to make that person well. Sometimes that person gets better, but sometimes he or she doesn't. Doesn't your god say he'll answer your prayers?"

"Yes, but sometimes the answer is 'No.' Just because it's something I want doesn't mean it's what's best overall."

Alvie frowned. "Then why even pray? Why would you put your trust in an entity that doesn't always answer your prayers yet says all you have to do is pray about something, and he'll make it happen. Isn't that a lie? I mean, doesn't the Bible tell you…what is it…oh, yes, 'I am the truth and the light' and 'ask and you shall receive'?"

"God has a plan for everyone and everything, and we can't change that."

"Then why do you ask him to?"

"Because if my faith is strong enough, God will consider making things go my way."

"Not if he already has a plan. You know from recent personal experience that one little change can affect the entire future of humankind."

Rene wrung her hands and looked away from Alvie. "I was raised to believe that God would do the best He can for me—that He knows what's better for me than I do. I was also taught that being a good person and believing in God is the best way to ensure that He'll love me and care for me and all those who turn to Him in their times of need. It also means I'll have a place in Heaven."

"So if you're a good person and you believe in God and you need a new Frigidaire, you can ask him for one and he'll give it to you without question?"

She closed her eyes and took a deep breath. "He won't just *give* it to me. He'll make things happen that will allow me to get one." She was getting frustrated.

"I understand your frustration," Alvie said, his voice soft and calm. "But think about this: if you had been born in another country…let's say India…chances are you wouldn't believe in or pray to the same god you do now. Does that mean you think all of those people—and there are a whole lot more of them than there are you—are wrong?"

"I was taught that they are unfortunate for believing in something—someone—other than God. That's why we send missionaries to other countries to show them the right way."

"So you solicit for your god?"

"Oh, Alvie, it's not solicitation. It's showing them the right path to take for salvation."

"And the benefit you reap from salvation is what? Heaven?"

"Yes, and eternal life there."

Alvie looked at her as if he had never seen her before. "Oolanaloo has granted you eternal life. I can't believe you're willing to forsake the purity, the absoluteness, the…the undeniable reality of Oolanaloo for something you've never had the opportunity to become one with. You say you talk to your god, but does he communicate with you in the same way Oolanaloo did?"

"I talk to God and know, in my heart, that He hears me and will do whatever is best for me."

"No!" Alvie said, turning his back to her and walking away, his voice ripe with irritation. "You have been told, throughout your entire life, that that's what you're *supposed* to do. It's the way you're *supposed* to feel. You've been goaded into thinking that's the right thing. But…" He turned back toward her but stopped short. It would have been evident to anyone that she was no longer sharing the room with Alvie mentally, only physically. Her eyes were closed, and her expression was one of distant serenity. She was with Oolanaloo.

Alvie watched her, and after a couple of moments, Rene opened her eyes and said, "I feel so much better now about…" her face was glowing.

"About what?" Alvie asked quietly.

"About life. About myself, my feelings." She turned toward him. "About us and our life together. It all makes perfect sense now."

"Oolanaloo can do that for you if you're willing to accept everything as it is."

"I know that now." She was still smiling. "I feel such a wonderful calmness. And a deep understanding of…"

"Of…?" Alvie prodded her.

"…of everything I've ever had doubts about."

"Isn't it a fantastic feeling? Like a weight has been lifted from your shoulders?"

She looked off into the distance. "The weight of the world. Of the universe." She looked back at Alvie. "I completely understand."

"Tell me about what you understand," Alvie said.

"Oolanaloo said my faith has been good, but my beliefs have been misguided. I didn't grasp that at first; I've always thought faith and belief were the same thing. But I was wrong. Oolanaloo explained that every living creature has faith. Even a lowly worm has faith that there will be something to eat if it continues to look for it. But it doesn't have beliefs; it was never taught to believe in something."

"I think the key word there is 'taught,' Alvie said. "Not too long ago you told me, and wisely I might add, that not all learning is the result of being taught, but that we learn more by experience. I'm sure Oolanaloo must have tried to make me recognize that somewhere along the line. But I just didn't grasp the concept. Like you, I guess I thought faith and belief were the same."

Rene said, "People use them interchangeably, but the actual

definitions are different. I understand that now."

"Thanks to you, so do I." Alvie pulled Rene close to him, embracing her as he would a small child. She closed her eyes as she felt him envelope her with his warmth, his tenderness, his total unconditional love for her. They remained in that embrace for several unwavering seconds, and both of them seemed to bask in the delight of it.

TWO SPECIAL HOLIDAYS

November came in with a bang, bringing with it twenty-nine inches of snow in less than twenty-four hours. But the people of Grand Marais simply shoveled themselves out and went about their daily business, Rene and Alvie among them. The temperatures remained below freezing for the rest of the month, and the snow continued to pile up.

November 20 marked the beginning of the Nuremberg War Crimes tribunal. A film titled "Nazi Concentration Camps" was screened on November 29, and the following day, witness Erwin von Lahousen testified that Keitel and von Ribbentrop gave orders for the murder of Poles, Jews, and Russian POWs. The prohibition against marriages between GIs and Austrian women was rescinded on November 29 and was later rescinded for German women, as well. Negro soldiers who served in the Army, in the case that they remained in the Army, were not allowed to marry white women (until 1948 when the prohibition against interracial marriages was removed).

On Thanksgiving Day, the sun came out and managed to lift everyone's spirits, though the cold persisted with the temperature not even reaching the low twenties. "I like the idea of a Thanksgiving covered-dish meal," Rene said. It was being held at the Coast Guard station. There were a great number of people in Grand Marais who no longer had children or other relatives living at home or even living close enough to visit on holidays, so the idea of being able to get together with one another for a celebration appealed to many of them. Rene was busy frosting the last of the cupcakes she had been baking for two days for the event. "Maybe it'll become an annual thing. It gives couples like us a place to go to socialize."

"And eat," Alvie added. Rene always teased him about how he considered eating a sport, as he had been unaware how wonderful food could be until he became human. And Alvie said it was difficult for him to remember when he hadn't eaten at all. "You've been saving up sugar for months, haven't you?" Alvie asked.

Rene nodded, her tongue unconsciously mimicking the route of the knife she was using to spread the icing around the top of one of the cupcakes. Alvie watched her and finally could no longer suppress his laughter.

"What's so funny?"

"I'm getting a real kick out of your tongue working just as hard as the knife to ice those cupcakes."

Rene looked at him like he was crazy. "My tongue?"

Alvie laughed again. "You probably aren't even aware you're doing it."

"Doing what?"

Alvie mimed frosting a cupcake and made a point of exaggerating the movements of his tongue while performing the act.

Rene blushed. "I didn't know I was doing that. Do I do that when I do other things?"

"Uh-huh. I love it. It's one of the things that makes you, you."

At around 11:30 a.m. they loaded the car with the boxes of cupcakes and went to the Coast Guard Station where several others had begun to gather. All were putting their favorite recipes out on long tables that had been arranged and covered with white tablecloths. The plan was to pass the food just like it would be done if the meal were taking place at each person's own home. Rene had been on the planning committee, and they all agreed that her idea of serving the food homestyle was much more personal than having a buffet.

Nearly forty people showed up with mounds of mashed potatoes, candied sweet potatoes, green beans, wax beans, baked beans, creamed corn, buttered turnips, Brussels sprouts with bacon, mashed rutabagas, potato salad, cranberry salad, and gelatin salads of all flavors and colors. The Coast Guard had taken the responsibility of roasting six stuffed turkeys, so there was plenty of stuffing (even some oyster dressing!) and gravy to accompany the meal. In spite of sugar rationing, there were several pumpkin and custard pies, a couple of cakes, lots of cookies, and Rene's cupcakes for dessert. No one went home hungry, and not one person left without expressing appreciation for all the work that had gone into the event, as well as plans to attend next Thanksgiving.

The weather didn't change between Thanksgiving and Christmas with the exception of more snow. By the time late December rolled around, there was just less than four feet on the level, but the piles of shoveled snow beside driveways and the piles that had been pushed up by the plows on the streets were over everyone's heads, even people as tall as Rene. There were no open sidewalks—some of the businesses had had to create tunnels to their store-front doors—and everyone was forced to walk from place-to-place via the street.

"It's fun to have a Christmas like this again," Rene said to Alvie, a wide grin lighting up her face.

"I love that you love it," Alvie said. "It makes me feel all warm and fuzzy inside. How long has it been since there was this much snow at Christmas?"

"Well, let me think," Rene said. She pursed her lips and closed one eye.

"I can almost see the wheels turning in that lovely head of yours."

Rene's face returned to normal, and she said, "It think it was in early 1927. January. It was shortly after you got here."

"I don't remember it," Alvie said, dejection showing on his face.

"You weren't around a lot that first year—you were going in and out all the time—so you probably missed it. I remember it didn't last very long because a warm spell moved in at the end of the month."

"I guess this is a first for me, then," he said.

"Yeah, I guess it is. I remember having a lot more snow

when I was a kid. And I remember winter lasting a lot longer, too. I wonder if that's the way all kids remember winter."

"I hope that's the case," Alvie said, a sad note in his voice. "Those were happy times for you."

"Do you miss never having been a kid?"

"I never really did until I met you. You've introduced me to more feelings and opportunities than I ever imagined possible. Even Oolanaloo commented on that fact when I chose to present myself to you as a young boy."

"That was a true moment of genius," Rene said, "and I'll never be able to thank you enough."

"Well, you have eternity to try."

On Christmas Day, Rene and Alvie exchanged gifts, nothing extraordinary, just personal items. They had bought a Christmas tree from a guy who came into town and set up a tree sales location in the empty lot beside the filling station. The tree was small, less than five feet tall, and began losing its needles on the day after they decorated it. But Rene said it made the house smell like Christmas, so she didn't care if she had to water it and sweep around it every day. Alvie insisted that she not spend all day fixing a special meal, so they ended up eating some leftovers and drinking a bottle of red wine Alvie had bought for the special day. They sat in front of a gently crackling fire, Rene's head on Alvie's shoulder.

"This is nice," Rene said, heaving a big, contented sigh. Alvie was absentmindedly fondling her hair. They both drifted off to sleep in the warmth of the fireplace.

Then it happened: Alvie's eyes popped open, and Rene sat straight up as if she'd been jolted by an electrical shock. They looked at each other, wide-eyed, mouths agape, and their eyes slowly drifted toward the ceiling.

Footsteps in the attic…

ENDNOTES

Chapter: **1918**
[1]Alfred Nobel
[2]Ray Kroc

Chapter: **1927**
[3]Amelia Earhart
[4]Albert Einstein
[5]Albert Einstein
[6]Albert Einstein

Chapter: **1928**
[7]Aesop
[8]Mahatma Gandhi
[9]An Wang
[10]A Jewish Proverb

Chapter: **1936**
[11]Henry Miller
[12]Mahatma Gandhi
[13]A man named William Donahey, writer and artist, created a cartoon called "The Teenie Weenies" that debuted in *The Chicago Tribune* in 1914. It was widely syndicated and was about tiny people (two inches tall) who lived in a pickle barrel under a rose bush. Their life took place among life-sized objects that, to them, appeared enormous. In 1926 Donahey surprised his wife, Mary, with a full-sized replica of that house, which he built for use as a summer cabin at Grand Sable Lake. It was a scaled-up model of the miniature oak casks that held Monarch-brand pickles. He

and Mary (also an author) used the cabin as inspiration for their writings. It was moved to downtown Grand Marais in 1936 after new tenants took possession of it. Over the years it has been an ice-cream stand, an information booth, and a souvenir shop. But it began to deteriorate until the Grand Marais Historical Society acquired the property in 2003 and restored it to its original condition. It now shows how the Donaheys lived there during the 1920s and 1930s.

[14]Arianna Huffington

Chapter **1942**
[15]Martin Luther King, Jr.
[16]Yehuda HaLevi (1075-1141)

Chapter **1943 – January**
[17]In 1939 the German authorities began to concentrate Poland's population of Jews (over three million) into ghettos throughout Poland's cities, Warsaw being the largest. During the summer of 1942, more than 250,000 Jews were taken from the Warsaw Ghetto to the Treblinka death camp where they were murdered. But even before the SS-controlled deportations to the extermination camps and the uprising in 1943, thousands died in the ghettos from disease and starvation.

The Jews who remained in Warsaw built bunkers and smuggled in weapons and explosives. Two groups (the left-wing faction, ŻOB, or Jewish Combat Organization and the right-wing faction, ŻZW, or Jewish Military Union) began a training program and put up the resistance effort in January, 1943, but it was only minimally successful. It did, however, ignite a spark in the Polish resistance groups to fervently pledge support to the Jews. The uprising was later deemed one of the most significant occurrences in the history of the Jewish people.

Members of the resistance movement initially chose not to fight the SS directives, thinking the Jews were being sent to labor camps instead of extermination camps. But they learned that all of the deported Jews were being murdered, and they decided to revolt; thus, the first armed resistance in the ghetto occurred in

January, 1943.

On Passover Eve, April 19, 1943, the Germans entered the Warsaw ghetto, and though the remaining Jews knew they would be murdered, they resisted. The surviving fighters escaped through the Muranowski tunnel and relocated in the Michalin forest. Thousands of remaining Jewish civilians took cover in the sewer system and multiple dugout hiding places among the ruins of the ghetto. But the Germans used dogs to sniff out the hideouts, then the Nazis dropped smoke bombs into the sewers to force the Jews from their hiding places. Sometimes the "bunkers" were destroyed by explosives, and sometimes there were shootouts, especially with the Germans who patrolled at night. Dozens of the remaining Jewish leaders and others ingested cyanide, committing mass suicide.

A Bundist member (a secular Jewish socialist) said in a farewell note prior to taking his own life, "I cannot continue to live and to be silent while the remnants of Polish Jewry, whose representative I am, are being murdered. My comrades in the Warsaw Ghetto fell with arms in their hands in the last heroic battle. I was not permitted to fall like them, together with them, but I belong with them, to my most profound protest against the inaction in which the world watches and permits the destruction of the Jewish people."

Thirteen-thousand Jews met their deaths within the ghetto during the uprising, six-thousand of whom were either burned alive or died from smoke inhalation. Fifty-thousand residents remained, but almost all were captured and transported to the Majdanek and Treblinka death camps. At the same time, The Bermuda Conference was being held (by the Allies) to discuss the Jewish refugees who had been liberated by Allied forces but still remained within German-occupied Europe.

In May, 1943, the Warsaw Ghetto uprising was terminated by blowing up the Warsaw Synagogue. The former ghetto is now completely destroyed except for eight buildings. German casualties amounted to a total of between 110 and 300 (based on which estimate is considered more official); however, for the sake of propaganda, the Germans announced that "only a few were wounded."

In 1944 prisoners from Auschwitz were forced to clear the remains of the ghetto. A few small groups of ghetto residents had been able to survive in the undetected bunkers. Several hundred survivors ended up taking part in the later uprising as members of the Polish Home Army and the Armia Ludowa.

In 1968, the 25th anniversary of the Warsaw Ghetto Uprising, Yitshak Zuckerman, a representative of the ŻOB on the 'Aryan' side and a founding member of the kibbutz Lohamei HaGeta'ot ("Ghetto Fighters") located north of Acre, Israel, said, "I don't think there's any real need to analyze the Uprising in military terms. This was a war of less than a thousand people against a mighty army and no one doubted how it was likely to turn out. This isn't a subject for study in military school. If there's a school to study the human spirit, there it should be a major subject. The important things were inherent in the force shown by Jewish youth after years of degradation, to rise up against their destroyers and determine what death they would choose: Treblinka or Uprising."

There exists a photograph of a young boy surrendering outside a bunker. His hands are in the air, and in the background are men holding submachine guns. It has become one of the best-known photos of the war and the Holocaust. The boy is said to represent all six million Jewish Holocaust victims.

Chapter 1943 – February through June
[18]Mitch Albom

[19]On the last day of April, near the Spanish coast, a body was released by Lt. Norman "Bill' Limbury Auchinleck Jewell's crew. False information had been planted on the man's body, which washed up on the shore of Spain where it was discovered by a local fisherman. That information misled the Germans about the site and timing of the Allied invasion of France. This became known as one of the most successful misinformation exercises of the war.

Dar Bagby

Chapter **1943 – July**
[20]John Wooden

Chapter **1944**
[21]The Katyn Massacre was a series of mass executions of approximately 8,000 Polish military officers imprisoned during the 1939 Soviet invasion of Poland, along with 6,000 police officers and another 8,000 intelligence agents, gendarmes, landowners, saboteurs, factory owners, lawyers, officials, and priests. The murdered consisted of ethnic Poles, Polish Ukranians, Belarusians, and Polish Jews, including Baruch Steinberg, Chief Rabbi of the Polish Army. The government of Nazi Germany discovered mass graves in the Katyn Forest in April, 1943, accusing the Soviets of committing the murders. Stalin vehemently denied any part in the affair and asked for an investigation by the International Committee of the Red Cross; the USSR claimed the victims had been killed by the Nazis and continued to deny responsibility for the massacres until 1990, when it officially acknowledged and condemned the killings by the NKVD (the *People's Commissariat for Internal Affairs*, the interior ministry of the Soviet Union) and the subsequent cover-up by the Soviet government.
[22]Max Lucado ("A man who wants to lead the orchestra must turn his back on the crowd.")
[23]Operation Ichi-Go ("Operation Number One") consisted of major battles between the Imperial Japanese Army and the National Revolutionary Army of the Republic of China. From April to December of 1944, three separate battles in the Chinese provinces of Henan, Hunan, and Guangxi were fought so that the Japanese could capture air bases in southeast China from which American bombers were attacking the Japanese, specifically shipping and their homeland. The Chinese front deteriorated rapidly after Operation Ichi-Go was launched, and FDR sent an ultimatum to Chaing Kai-shek (China's leader) threatening to end all American aid unless General Joseph Stilwell was placed in unrestricted command of all of Chiang's forces, to which he agreed. As a result, Japanese attempts failed, and Japan

was no closer to defeating China after the operation. The Japanese suffered 11,742 killed in action by mid-November, but the number of Japanese who died of illness was more than double that number.

The 1958 novel *The Mountain Road* by Theodore White (a "Time Magazine" correspondent in China during the Operation Ichi-Go offensive) was based on an interview with former OSS Major Frank Gleason whose soldiers blew up anything that had been left behind in the retreat by the Japanese. They ultimately destroyed over 150 bridges and 50,000 tons of munitions. James Stewart, star of a film adaptation of the event, was actually opposed to war films due to their inaccuracy, but because this film was anti-war, it was the only one in which he agreed to play a soldier.

Chapter 1945 – January through June

[24]The "Manila Massacre" (aka, "The Rape of Manila") occurred in the capital of the Philippines during the Battle of Manila from February 3, 1945, to March 3, 1945. Committed against Filipino civilians by the Imperial Japanese Army troops, it was considered one of several major war crimes, as judged by the postwar military tribunal. Approximately 100,000 civilians were killed during the incident.

The Japanese commanding general, Tomoyuki Yamashita, decided he would be unable to defend Manila with his available forces, so he insisted on a complete withdrawal of the troops in January, 1945. His order, however, was ignored by about 10,000 Japanese marines (under Rear Admiral Sanji Iwabuchi). The Japanese issued the following order justifying the Manila massacre: "The Americans who have penetrated into Manila have about 1000 troops, and there are several thousand Filipino soldiers under the Commonwealth Army and the organized guerrillas. Even women and children have become guerrillas. All people on the battlefield with the exception of Japanese military personnel, Japanese civilians, and special construction units will be put to death."

The United States Army advanced into Manila to drive the

Japanese out, but during lulls in the battle to control the city, the Japanese troops retaliated on Manila's civilians with violent rapes, mutilations, and massacres in schools, hospitals, and convents. They forced Filipino women and children to be used as human shields to protect them on the front lines; any who survived were then murdered by the Japanese.

In order to clear north Manila of guerrillas, the Japanese executed 54,000+ Filipinos, including children, as they passed through towns doing mop-up operations. Pregnant Filipino women's bellies were ripped open, and the women were murdered. Four hundred women and girls were rounded up from the Ermita district (Manila's wealthy) and submitted to a selection board that picked out the twenty-five most beautiful, many only 12 to 14 years old. These were taken to the Bayview Hotel—the designated "rape center"—where Japanese enlisted men took turns raping them.

Japanese soldiers entered a German club where allied Germans were taking refuge. The Japanese soldiers bayoneted infants and children while their mothers pled for mercy, and at least twenty of the soldiers raped a young girl before slicing off her breasts, after which one of the soldiers placed her mutilated breasts on his chest, mimicking a woman, while the other Japanese soldiers laughed. Then they doused the young girl, and two other women who had been raped to death, in gasoline and set them all on fire. The soldiers eventually set the entire club on fire, killing many of the inhabitants, but the ones caught while trying to escape were raped and had their hair set on fire. One was partially decapitated after an attempt to defend herself.

Though Rear Admiral Iwabuchi's marines committed the atrocities, and though General Yamashita had ordered him to evacuate Manila prior to the massacre, Yamashita was the one who was convicted as a war criminal. There was no evidence that the general participated in the actual crimes, ordered others to do so, was in a position to prevent them, or even suspected they were about to happen. But the Supreme Court of the United States (consisting of six U.S. generals, including MacArthur) held Yamashita responsible because he was in command of all the Japanese troops in the Philippines at the time of the massacre. He was sentenced to death by hanging, despite a group of military lawyers who attempted to defend General Yamashita by appealing to the U.S. Supreme Court, calling the trial a "miscarriage of justice, an exercise in vengeance, and a denial of human rights." But the appeal failed, and the general was hanged on February 23, 1946, in Manila.

Chapter **1945 – July through December**
[25]Robert Frost

CPSIA information can be obtained
at www.ICGtesting.com
Printed in the USA
JSHW042359070221
11529JS00002B/5